Ten years ago, bestselling romance author
Diana Palmer launched Silhouette Desire's very first
MAN OF THE MONTH with her classic, heartfelt
story *Reluctant Father* (SD #469, 1/89).

Now, in celebration of a decade of unforgettable,
irresistible men, Silhouette Desire brings you a very
special anniversary book, the January 1999
MAN OF THE MONTH,

BELOVED
by
DIANA PALMER

Meet Simon Hart: He's gruff and gorgeous...and
not about to let his guard down and fall for a
headstrong socialite, no matter how enticingly
innocent she might be. But this lady had always
secretly loved Simon, and now this Long, Tall
Texan was about to become her beloved....

"Nobody tops Diana Palmer...I love her stories."
—*New York Times* Bestselling Author
Jayne Ann Krentz

MEN of the YEAR

Dear Reader,

Welcome to a new year with Silhouette Desire! We begin the year in celebration—it's the 10th Anniversary of MAN OF THE MONTH! And kicking off the festivities is the incomparable Diana Palmer, with January's irresistible hero, Simon Hart, in *Beloved*.

Also launching this month is Desire's series FORTUNE'S CHILDREN: THE BRIDES. So many of you wrote to us that you loved Silhouette's series FORTUNE'S CHILDREN—now here's a whole new branch of the family! Award-winning author Jennifer Greene inaugurates this series with *The Honor Bound Groom*.

Popular Anne Marie Winston begins BUTLER COUNTY BRIDES, a new miniseries about three small-town friends who find true love, with *The Baby Consultant*. Sara Orwig offers us a marriage of convenience in *The Cowboy's Seductive Proposal*. Next, experience love on a ranch in *Hart's Baby* by Christy Lockhart. And opposites attract in *The Scandalous Heiress* by Kathryn Taylor.

So, indulge yourself in 1999 with Silhouette Desire—powerful, provocative and passionate love stories that speak to today's multifaceted woman. Each month we offer you six compelling romances to meet your many moods, with heroines you'll care about and heroes to die for. Silhouette Desire is everything *you* desire in a romance novel.

Enjoy!

Joan Marlow Golan
Senior Editor, Silhouette Desire

Please address questions and book requests to:
Silhouette Reader Service
U.S.: 3010 Walden Ave., P.O. Box 1325, Buffalo, NY 14269
Canadian: P.O. Box 609, Fort Erie, Ont. L2A 5X3

DIANA PALMER
BELOVED

SILHOUETTE *Desire*

Published by Silhouette Books

America's Publisher of Contemporary Romance

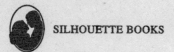

SILHOUETTE BOOKS

ISBN 0-373-76189-9

BELOVED

Printed in U.S.A.

To Debbie and the staff at Books Galore,
in Watkinsville, GA.
and to all my wonderful readers there and in Athens.

Prologue

Simon Hart sat alone in the second row of the seats reserved for family. He wasn't really kin to John Beck, but the two had been best friends since college. John had been his only real friend. Now he was dead, and there *she* sat like a dark angel, her titian hair veiled in black, pretending to mourn the husband she'd cast off like a worn coat after only a month of marriage.

He crossed his long legs, shifting uncomfortably against the pew. He had an ache where his left arm ended just at the elbow. The sleeve was pinned, because he hated the prosthesis that disguised his handicap. He was handsome enough even with only one arm—he had thick, wavy black hair on a leonine head, with dark eyebrows and pale gray eyes. He was tall and well built, a dynamo of a man; former state attorney general of Texas and a nationally known trial lawyer, in addition to being one of the owners of the Hart ranch properties, which were worth millions. He and his brothers were as famous in cattle circles as Simon was in legal circles. He was filthy rich and looked it. But the money didn't make up for the loneliness. His wife had died in the accident that took his arm. It had happened just after Tira's marriage to John Beck.

Tira had nursed him in the hospital, and gossip had run rampant. Simon was alluded to as the cause of the divorce. Stupid idea, he thought angrily, because he wouldn't have had Tira on a bun with catsup. Only a week after the divorce, she was seen everywhere with playboy Charles Percy, who was still her closest companion. He was probably her lover, as well, Simon thought with suppressed fury. He liked Percy no better than he liked Tira. Strange that Percy hadn't come to the funeral, but perhaps he did have some sense of decency, however small.

Simon wondered if Tira realized how he really felt about her. He had to be pleasant to her; anything else would have invited comment. But secretly, he despised her for what she'd done to John. Tira was cold inside—selfish and cold and unfeeling. Otherwise, how could she have turned John out after a month of marriage, and then let him go to work on a dangerous oil rig in the North Atlantic in an attempt to forget her? John had died there this week, in a tragic accident, having drowned in the freezing, churning waters before he could be rescued. Simon couldn't help thinking that John wanted to die. The letters he'd had from his friend were full of his misery, his loneliness, his isolation from love and happiness.

He glared in her direction, wondering how John's father could bear to sit beside her like that, holding her slender hand as if he felt as sorry for her as he felt for himself at the loss of his son, his only child. Putting on a show for the public, he concluded irritably. He was pretending, to keep people from gossiping.

Simon stared at the closed casket and winced. It was like the end of an era for him. First he'd lost Melia, his wife, and his arm; now he'd lost John, too. He had wealth and success, but no one to share it with. He wondered if Tira felt any guilt for what she'd done to John. He couldn't imagine that she did. She was always flamboyant, vivacious, outgoing and mercurial. Simon had watched her without her knowing it, hating himself for what he felt when he looked at her. She was tall, beautiful, with long, glorious red-gold hair that went to her waist, pale green eyes and a figure right out of a fashion magazine. She could have been a model, but she was surprisingly shy for a pretty woman.

Simon had already been married when they met, and it had been at his prompting that John had taken Tira out for the first time. He'd thought they were compatible, both rich and pleasant people. It had seemed a marriage made in heaven; until the quick divorce. Simon would never have admitted that he threw Tira together with John to get her out of his own circle and out of the reach of temptation. He told himself that she was everything he despised in a woman, the sort of person he could never care for. It worked, sometimes. Except for the ache he felt every time he saw her; an ache that wasn't completely physical....

When the funeral service was over, Tira went out with John's father holding her elbow. The older man smiled sympathetically at Simon. Tira didn't look at him. She was really crying; he could see it even through the veil

Good, Simon thought with cold vengeance. *Good, I'm glad it's hurt you. You killed him, after all!*

He didn't look her way as he got into his black limousine and drove himself back to the office. He wasn't going to the graveside service. He'd had all of Tira's pathetic charade that he could stand. He wouldn't think about those tears in her tragic eyes, or the genuine sadness in her white face. He wouldn't think about her guilt or his own anger. It was better to put it all in the past and let it lie, forgotten. If he could. If he *could....*

One

The numbered lot of Hereford cattle at this San Antonio auction had been a real steal at the price, but Tira Beck had let it go without a murmur to the man beside her. She wouldn't ever have admitted that she didn't need to add to her substantial Montana cattle herd, which was managed by her foreman, since she lived in Texas. She'd only wanted to attend the auction because she knew Simon Hart was going to be there. Usually his four brothers in Jacobsville, Texas, handled cattle sales. But Simon, like Tira, lived in San Antonio where the auction was being held, so it seemed natural to let him make the bids.

He wasn't a rancher anymore. He was still tall and well built, with broad shoulders and a leonine head topped by thick black wavy hair. But the empty sleeve on his left side attested to the fact that his days of working cattle were pretty much over. It didn't affect his ability to make a living, at least. He was a former state attorney general and a nationally famous trial attorney who could pick and choose high-profile cases. He made a substantial wage. His voice was still his best asset, a deep velvety one that projected well in a courtroom. In addition to that was a dangerously deceptive manner that lulled witnesses into a false sense of security before he cut them to pieces on the stand. He had a verbal killer instinct, and he used it to good effect.

Tira, on the other hand, lived a hectic life doing charity work and was independently wealthy. She was a divorcée who had very little to do with men except on a platonic basis. There weren't many friends, either. Simon Hart and Charles Percy were the lot, and Charles was hopelessly in love with his brother's wife. She was the only person who knew that. Many people thought that she and Charles were lovers, which amused them both. She had her own secrets to keep. It suited her purposes to keep Simon in the dark about her emotional state.

"That was a hell of an anemic bid you made," Simon remarked as the next lot of cattle were led into the sale ring. "What's wrong with you today?"

"My heart's not in it," she replied. "I haven't had a lot to do with the Montana ranch since Dad died. I've given some thought to selling the property. I'll never live there again."

"You'll never sell. You have too many attachments to the ranch. Besides, you've got a good manager in place up there," he said pointedly.

She shrugged, pushing away a wisp of glorious hair that had escaped from the elegant French twist at her nape. "So I have."

"But you'd rather swan around San Antonio with Charles Percy," he murmured, his chiseled mouth twisting into a mocking smile.

She glanced at him with lovely green eyes and hid a carefully concealed hope that he might be jealous. But his expression gave no hint of his feelings. Neither did those pale gray eyes under thick black eyebrows. It was the same old story. The wreck eight years ago that had cost him his arm had also cost him his beloved wife, Melia. Despite their differences, no one had doubted his love for her. He hadn't been serious about a woman since her death, although he escorted his share of sophisticated women to local social events.

"What's the matter?" he asked when his sharp eyes caught her disappointment.

She shrugged in her elegant black pantsuit. "Oh, nothing. I just thought that you might like to stand up and threaten to kill Charles if he came near me again." She glanced at his shocked face and chuckled. "I'm kidding!" she chided.

His gaze cut into hers for a second and then they moved back to the sale ring. "You're in an odd mood today."

She sighed, returning her attention to the program in her beautifully manicured hands. "I've been in an odd mood for years. Not that I ever expect you to notice."

He closed his own program with a snap and glared down at her. "That's another thing that annoys me, those throwaway remarks you make. If you want to say something to me, just come out and say it."

Typically blunt, she thought. She looked straight at him and she made a gesture of utter futility with one hand. "Why bother?" she asked. Her eyes searched his and for the first time, a hint of the pain she felt was visible. She averted her gaze and stood up. "I've done all the bidding I came to do. I'll see you around, Simon."

She picked up her long black leather coat and folded it over her arm as she made her way out of the row and up the aisle to the exit. Eyes followed her, and not only because she was one of only a handful of women present. Tira was beautiful, although she never paid the least attention to her appearance except with a critical scrutiny. She wasn't vain.

Behind her, Simon sat scowling silently as she walked away. Her behavior piqued his curiosity. She was even more remote lately and hardly the same flamboyant, cheerful, friendly woman who'd been his secret solace since the accident that had cost Melia her life. His wife had been his whole heart, until that last night when she betrayed a secret that destroyed his pride and his love for her.

Fool that he was, he'd believed that Melia married him for love. In fact, she'd married him for money and kept a lover in the background. Her stark confession about her long-standing affair and the abortion of his child had shocked and wounded him. She'd even laughed at his consternation. Surely he didn't think she wanted a child? It would have ruined her figure and her social life. Besides, she'd added with calculating cruelty, she hadn't even been certain that it was Simon's, since she'd been with her lover during the same period of time.

The truth had cut like a knife into his pride. He'd taken his eyes off the road as they argued, and hit a patch of black ice on that winter evening. The car had gone off the road into a gulley and Melia, who had always refused to wear a seat belt because they were uncomfortable to her, had been thrown into the windshield headfirst. She'd died instantly. Simon had been luckier, but the airbag on his side of the car hadn't deployed, and the impact of the crash had driven the metal of the door right into his left arm. Amputation had been necessary to save his life.

He remembered that Tira had come to him in the hospital as soon as she'd heard about the wreck. She'd been in the process of divorcing John Beck, her husband, and her presence at Simon's side had started some malicious rumors about infidelity.

Tira never spoke of her brief marriage. She never spoke of John. Simon had already been married when they'd met for the first time, and it had been Simon who played matchmaker with John for her. John was his best friend and very wealthy, like Tira herself, and they seemed to have much in common. But the marriage had been over in less than a month.

He'd never questioned why, except that it seemed unlike Tira to throw in the towel so soon. Her lack of commitment to her marriage and her cavalier attitude about the divorce had made him uneasy. In fact, it had kept him from letting her come closer after he was widowed. She'd turned out to be shallow, and he wasn't risking his heart on a woman like that, even if she was a knockout to look at. As he knew firsthand, there was more to a marriage than having a beautiful wife.

John Beck, like Tira, had never said anything about the marriage. But John had avoided Simon ever since the divorce, and once when he'd had too much to drink at a party they'd both attended, he'd blurted out that Simon had destroyed his life, without explaining how. The two men had been friends for several years until

John had married Tira. Not too long after the divorce, John had moved out of Texas entirely and a year later that tragic oil rig accident had claimed his life. Tira had seemed devastated by John's death and for a time, she went into seclusion. When she came back into society, she was a changed woman. The vivacious, happy Tira of earlier days had become a dignified, elegant matron who seemed to have lost her fighting spirit. She went back to college and finished her degree in art. But three years after graduation, she seemed to have done little with her degree. Not that she skimped on charity work or political fund-raising. She was a tireless worker. Simon wondered sometimes if she didn't work to keep from thinking.

Perhaps she blamed herself for John's death and couldn't admit it. The loss of his former friend had hurt Simon, too. He and Tira had become casual friends, but nothing more, he made sure of it. Despite her attractions, he wasn't getting caught by such a shallow woman. But if their lukewarm friendship had been satisfying once, in the past year, she'd become restless. She was forever mentioning Charles Percy to him and watching his reactions with strange, curious eyes. It made him uncomfortable, like that crack she'd made about kindling jealousy in him.

That remark hit him on the raw. Did she really think he could ever want a woman of her sort, who could discard a man she professed to love after only one month of marriage and then parade around openly with a philanderer like Charles Percy? He laughed coldly to himself. That really would be the day. His heart was safely encased in ice. Everyone thought he mourned Melia—no one knew how badly she'd hurt him, or that her memory disgusted him. It served as some protection against women like Tira. It kept him safe from any emotional involvement.

Unaware of Simon's hostile thoughts, Tira went to her silver Jaguar and climbed in behind the wheel. She paused there for a few minutes, with her head against the cold steering wheel. When was she ever going to learn that Simon didn't want her? It was like throwing herself at a stone wall, and it had to stop. Finally she admitted that nothing was going to change their shallow relationship. It was time she made a move to put herself out of Simon's orbit for good. Tearing her emotions to pieces wasn't going to help, and every time she saw him, she died a little more. All these years she'd waited and hoped and suffered, just to be around him occasionally. She'd lived too long on crumbs; she had to find some sort of life for herself without Simon, no matter how badly it hurt.

Her first step was to sell the Montana property. She put it on the market without a qualm, and her manager pooled his resources with a friend to buy it. With the ranch gone, she had no more reason to go to cattle auctions.

She moved out of her apartment that was only a couple of blocks from Simon's, too, and bought an elegant house on the outskirts of town on the Floresville Road. It was very Spanish, with graceful arches and black wrought-iron scrollwork on the fences that enclosed it. There was a cobblestone patio complete with a fountain and a nearby sitting area with a large goldfish pond and a waterfall cascading into it. The place was sheer magic. She thought she'd never seen anything quite so beautiful.

"It's the sort of house that needs a family," the real estate agent had remarked.

Tira hadn't said a word.

She remembered the conversation as she looked around the empty living room that had yet to be furnished. There would never be a family now. There would only be Tira, putting one foot in front of the other and living like a zombie in a world that no longer contained Simon, or hope.

It took her several weeks to have the house decorated and furnished. She chose every fabric, every color, every design herself. And when the house was finished, it echoed her own personality. Her real personality, that was, not the face she showed to the world.

No one who was acquainted with her would recognize her from the decor. The living room was done in soft white with a pastel blue, patterned wallpaper. The carpet was gray. The furniture was Victorian, rosewood chairs and a velvet-covered sofa. The other rooms were equally antique. The master bedroom boasted a four-poster bed in cherry wood, with huge ball legs and a headboard and footboard resplendant with hand-carved floral motifs. The curtains were Priscillas, the center panels of rose patterns with faint pink and blue coloring. The rest of the house followed the same subdued elegance of style and color. It denoted a person who was introverted, sensitive and old-fashioned. Which, under the flamboyant camouflage, Tira really was.

If there was a flaw, and it was a small one, it was the mouse who lived in the kitchen. Once the house was finished, and she'd moved in, she noticed him her first night in residence, sitting brazenly on a cabinet clutching a piece of cracker that she'd missed when she was cleaning up.

She bought traps and set them, hoping that the evil things would do their horrible work correctly and that she wouldn't be left nursing a wounded mouse. But the wily creature avoided the traps. She tried a cage and bait. That didn't work, either. Either the mouse was like those in that cartoon she'd loved, altered by some secret lab and made intelligent, or he was a figment of her imagination and she was going mad.

She laughed almost hysterically at the thought that Simon had finally, after all those years, driven her crazy.

Despite the mouse, she loved her new home. But even though she led a hectic life, there were still the lonely nights to get through. The walls began to close around her, despite the fact that she involved herself in charity work committees and was a tireless worker for political action fund-raisers. She worked long hours, and pushed herself unnecessarily hard. But she had no outside interests and too much money to work a daily job. What she needed was something interesting to do at home, to keep her mind occupied at night, when she was alone. But what?

It was a rainy Monday morning. She'd gone to the market for fresh vegetables and wasn't really watching where she was walking when she turned a corner and went right into the path of Corrigan Hart and his new wife, Dorothy.

"Good Lord," she gasped, catching her breath. "What are you two doing in San Antonio?"

Corrigan grinned. "Buying cattle," he said, drawing a radiant Dorothy closer. "Which reminds me, I didn't see you at the auction this time. I was standing in for Simon," he added. "For some reason, he's gone off sales lately."

"So have I, coincidentally," Tira remarked with a cool smile. It stung to think that Simon had given up those auctions that he loved so much to avoid her, but that was most certainly the reason. "I sold the Montana property."

Corrigan scowled. "But you loved the ranch. It was your last link with your father."

That was true, and it had made her sad for a time. She twisted the shopping basket in her hands. "I'd gotten into a rut," she said. "I wanted to change my life."

"So I noticed," Corrigan said quietly. "We went by your apartment to say hello. You weren't there."

"I moved." She colored a little at his probing glance. "I've bought a house across town."

Corrigan's eyes narrowed. "Someplace where you won't see Simon occasionally," he said gently.

The color in her cheeks intensified. "Where I won't see Simon at all, if you want the truth," she said bluntly. "I've given up all my connections with the past. There won't be any more accidental meetings with him. I've decided that I'm tired of eating my heart out for a man who doesn't want me. So I've stopped."

Corrigan looked surprised. Dorie eyed the other woman with quiet sympathy.

"In the long run, that's probably the best thing you could have done," Dorie said quietly. "You're still young and very pretty," she added with a smile. "And the world is full of men."

"Of course it is," Tira replied. She returned Dorie's smile. "I'm glad things worked out for you two, and

I'm very sorry I almost split you up," she added sincerely. "Believe me, it was unintentional."

"Tira, I know that," Dorie replied, remembering how a chance remark of Tira's in a local boutique had sent Dorie running scared from Corrigan. That was all in the past, now. "Corrigan explained everything to me. I was uncertain of him then, that's all it really was. I'm not anymore." She hesitated. "I'm sorry about you and Simon."

Tira's face tautened. "You can't make people love you," she said with a poignant sadness in her eyes. She shrugged fatalistically. "He has a life that suits him. I'm trying to find one for myself."

"Why don't you do a collection of sculptures and have a show?" Corrigan suggested.

She chuckled. "I haven't done sculpture in three years. Anyway, I'm not good enough for that."

"You certainly are, and you've got an art degree. Use it."

She considered that. After a minute, she smiled. "Well, I do enjoy sculpting. I used to sell some of it occasionally."

"See?" Corrigan said. "An idea presents itself." He paused. "Of course, there's always a course in biscuit-making…?"

Knowing his other three brothers' absolute mania for that particular bread, she held up both hands. "You can tell Leo and Cag and Rey that I have no plans to become a biscuit chef."

"I'll pass the message along. But Dorie's dying for a replacement," he added with a grin at his wife. "They'd chain her to the stove if I didn't intervene." He eyed Tira. "They like you."

"God forbid," she said with a mock shudder. "For

years, people will be talking about how they arranged your marriage.''

"They meant well," Dorie defended them.

"Baloney," Tira returned. "They had to have their biscuits. Fatal error, Dorie, telling them you could bake."

"It worked out well, though, don't you think?" she asked with a radiant smile at her husband.

"It did, indeed."

Tira fielded a few more comments about her withdrawal from the social scene, and then they were on their way to the checkout stand. She deliberately held back until they left, to avoid any more conversation. They were a lovely couple, and she was fond of Corrigan, but he reminded her too much of Simon.

In the following weeks, she signed up for a refresher sculpting course at her local community college, a course for no credit since she already had a degree. In no time, she was sculpting recognizable busts.

"You've got a gift for this," her instructor murmured as he walked around a fired head of her favorite movie star. "There's money in this sort of thing, you know. Big money."

She almost groaned aloud. How could she tell this dear man that she had too much money already? She only smiled and thanked him for the compliment.

But he put her sculpture in a showing of his students' work. It was seen by a local art gallery owner, who tracked Tira down and offered her an exclusive showing. She tried to dissuade him, but the offer was all too flattering to turn down. She agreed, with the priviso that the proceeds would go to an outreach program from the local hospital that worked in indigent neighborhoods.

After that, there was no stopping her. She spent hours at the task, building the strength in her hands and attuning her focus to more detailed pieces.

It wasn't until she finished one of Simon that she even realized she'd been sculpting him. She stared at it with contained fury and was just about to bring both fists down on top of it when the doorbell rang.

Irritated at the interruption, she tossed a cloth over the work in progress and went to answer it, wiping the clay from her hands on the way. Her hair was in a neat bun, to keep it from becoming clotted with clay, but her pink smock was liberally smeared with it. She looked a total mess, without makeup, even without shoes, wearing faded jeans and a knit top.

She opened the door without questioning who her visitor might be, and froze in place when Simon came into view on the porch. She noticed that he was wearing the prosthesis he hated so much, and she noted with interest that the hand at the end of it looked amazingly real.

She lifted her eyes to his, but her face wasn't welcoming. She didn't open the door to admit him. She didn't even smile.

"What do you want?" she asked.

He scowled. That was new. He'd visited Tira's apartment infrequently in the past, and he'd always been greeted with warmth and even delight. This was a cold reception indeed.

"I came to see how you were," he replied quietly. "You've been conspicuous by your absence around town lately."

"I sold the ranch," she said flatly.

He nodded. "Corrigan told me." He looked around at the front yard and the porch of the house. "This is nice. Did you really need a whole house?"

She ignored the question. "What do you want?" she asked again.

He noted her clay-smeared hands, and the smock she was wearing. "Laying bricks, are you?" he mused.

She didn't smile, as she might have once. "I'm sculpting."

"Yes, I remember that you took courses in college. You were quite good."

"I'm also quite busy," she said pointedly.

His eyebrow arched. "No invitation to have coffee?"

She hardened her resolve, despite the frantic beat of her heart. "I don't have time to entertain. I'm getting ready for an exhibit."

"At Bob Henderson's gallery," he said knowledgeably. "Yes, I know. I have part ownership in it." He held up his hand when she started to speak angrily. "I had no idea that he'd seen any of your work. I didn't suggest the showing. But I'd like to see what you've done. I do have a vested interest."

That put a new complexion on things. But she still didn't want him in her house. She'd never rid herself of the memory of him in it. Her reluctant expression told him that whatever she was feeling, it wasn't pleasure.

He sighed. "Tira, what's wrong?" he asked.

She stared at the cloth in her hands instead of at him. "Why does anything have to be wrong?"

"Are you kidding?" He drew in a heavy breath and wondered why he should suddenly feel guilty. "You've sold the ranch, moved house and given up any committees that would bring you into contact with me...."

She looked up in carefully arranged surprise. "Oh, heavens, it wasn't because of you," she lied convincingly. "I was in a rut, that's all. I decided that I needed to turn my life around. And I have."

His eyes glittered down at her. "Did turning it around include keeping me out of it?"

Her expression was unreadable. "I suppose it did. I was never able to get past my marriage. The memories were killing me, and you were a constant reminder."

His heavy eyebrows lifted. "Why should the memories bother you?" he asked with visible sarcasm. "You didn't give a damn about John. You divorced him a month after the wedding and never seemed to care if you saw him again or not. Barely a week later, you were keeping company with Charles Percy."

The bitterness in his voice opened her eyes to something she'd never seen. Why, he blamed her for John's death. She didn't seem to breathe as she looked up into those narrow, cold, accusing eyes. It had been three years since John's death and she'd never known that Simon felt this way.

Her hands on the cloth stilled. It was the last straw. She'd loved this big, formidable man since the first time she'd seen him. There had never been anyone else in her heart, despite the fact that she'd let him push her into marrying John. And now, years too late, she discovered the reason that Simon had never let her come close to him. It was the last reason she'd ever have guessed.

She let out a harsh breath. "Well," she said with forced lightness, "the things we learn about people we thought we knew!" She tucked the smeared cloth into a front pocket of her equally smeared smock. "So I killed John. Is that what you think, Simon?"

The frontal assault was unexpected. His guard was down and he didn't think before he spoke. "You played at marriage," he accused quietly. "He loved you, but you had nothing to give him. A month of marriage and you were having divorce papers served to him. You let him go without a word when he decided to work on oil rigs, despite the danger of it. You didn't even try to stop him. Funny, but I never realized what a shallow, cold woman you were until then. Everything you are is on the outside," he continued, blind to her white, drawn face. "Glorious hair, a pretty face, sparkling eyes, pretty figure...and nothing under it all. Not even a spark of compassion or love for anyone except yourself."

She wasn't breathing normally. Dear God, she thought, don't let me faint at his feet! She swallowed once, then twice, trying to absorb the horror of what he was saying to her.

"You never said a word," she said in a haunted tone. "In all these years."

"I didn't think it needed saying," he said simply. "We've been friends, of a sort. I hope we still are." He smiled, but it didn't reach his eyes. "As long as you realize that you'll never be allowed within striking distance of my heart. I'm not a masochist, even if John was."

Later, when she was alone, she was going to die. She knew it. But right now, pride spared her any further hurt.

She went past him, very calmly, and opened the front door, letting in a scent of dead leaves and cool October breeze. She didn't speak. She didn't look at him. She just stood there.

He walked past her, hesitating on the doorstep. His narrow eyes scanned what he could see of her face, and its whiteness shocked him. He wondered why she looked so torn up, when he was only speaking the truth.

Before he could say a thing, she closed the door, threw the dead bolt and put on the chain latch. She walked back toward her studio, vaguely aware that he was trying to call her back.

The next morning, the housekeeper she'd hired, Mrs. Lester, found her sprawled across her bed with a loaded pistol in her hands and an empty whiskey bottle lying on its side on the stained gray carpet. Mrs. Lester quickly looked in the bathroom and found an empty bottle that had contained tranquilizers. She jerked up the telephone and dialed the emergency services number with trembling hands. When the ambulance came screaming up to the front of the house, Tira still hadn't moved at all.

TWO

It took all of that day for Tira to come out of the stupor and discover where she was. It was a very nice hospital room, but she didn't remember how she'd gotten there. She was foggy and disoriented and very sick to her stomach.

Dr. Ron Gaines, an old family friend, came in the door ahead of a nurse in neat white slacks and a multicolored blouse with many pockets.

"Get her vitals," the doctor directed.

"Yes, sir."

While her temperature and blood pressure and pulse rate were taken, Dr. Gaines leaned against the wall quietly making notations on her chart. The nurse reported her findings, he charted them and he motioned her out of the room.

He moved to the bed and sat down in the chair beside Tira. "If anyone had asked me two weeks ago, I'd have said that you were the most levelheaded woman I knew. You've worked tirelessly for charities here, you've spearheaded fund drives... Good God, what's the matter with you?''

"I had a bad blow," she confessed in a subdued tone. "It was unexpected and I did something stupid. I got drunk."

"Don't hand me that! Your housekeeper found a loaded pistol in your hand."

"Oh, that." She started to tell him about the mouse, the one she'd tried unsuccessfully to catch for weeks. Last night, with half a bottle of whiskey in her, shooting the varmint had seemed perfectly logical. But her dizzy mind was slow to focus. "Well, you see—" she began.

He sighed heavily and cut her off. "Tira, if it wasn't a suicide attempt, I'm not a doctor. Tell me the truth."

She blinked. "I wouldn't try to kill myself!" she said, outraged. She took a slow breath. "I was just a little depressed, that's all. I found out yesterday that Simon holds me responsible for John's death."

There was a long, shocked pause. "He doesn't know why the marriage broke up?"

She shook her head.

"Why didn't you tell him, for God's sake?" he exclaimed.

"It isn't the sort of thing you tell a man about his best friend. I never dreamed that he blamed me. We've been friends. He never wanted it to be anything except friendship, and I assumed it was because of the way he felt about Melia. Apparently I've been five kinds of an idiot." She looked up at him. "Six, if you count last night," she added, flushing.

"I'm glad you agree that it was stupid."

She frowned. "Did you pump my stomach?"

"Yes."

"No wonder I feel so empty," she said. "Why did you do that?" she asked. "I only had whiskey on an empty stomach!"

"Your housekeeper found an empty tranquilizer bottle in the bathroom," he said sternly.

"Oh, that," she murmured. "The bottle was empty. I never throw anything away. That prescription was years old. It's one Dr. James gave me to get me through final exams in college three years ago. I was a nervous wreck!" She gave him another unblinking stare. "But you listen here, I'm not suicidal. I'm the least suicidal person I know. But everybody has a breaking point and I reached mine. So I got drunk. I never touch alcohol. Maybe that's why it hit me so hard."

He took her hand in his and held it gently. While he was trying to find the words, the door suddenly swung open and a wild-eyed Simon Hart entered the room. He looked as if he'd been in an accident, his face was so white. He stared at Tira without speaking.

It wasn't his fault, really, but she hated him for what she'd done to herself. Her eyes told him so. There was no welcome in them, no affection, no coquettishness. She looked at him as if she wished she had a weapon in her hands.

"You get out of my room!" she raged at him, sitting straight up in bed.

The doctor's eyebrows shot straight up. Tira had never raised her voice to Simon before. Her face was flaming red, like her wealth of hair, and her green eyes were shooting bolts of lightning in Simon's direction.

"Tira," Simon began uncertainly.

"Get out!" she repeated, ashamed of being accused

of a suicide attempt in the first place. It was bad enough that she'd lost control of herself enough to get drunk. She glared at Simon as if he was the cause of it all—which he was. "Out!" she repeated, when he didn't move, gesturing wildly with her arm.

He wouldn't go, and she burst into tears of frustrated fury. Dr. Gaines got between Simon and Tira and hit the Call button. "Get in here, stat," he said into the intercom, following the order with instructions for a narcotic. He glanced toward Simon, standing frozen in the doorway. "Out," he said without preamble. "I'll speak to you in a few minutes."

Simon moved aside to let the skurrying nurse into the room with a hypodermic. He could hear Tira's sobs even through the door. He moved a little way down the hall, to where his brother Corrigan was standing.

It had been Corrigan whom the housekeeper called when she discovered Tira. And he'd called Simon and told him only that Tira had been taken to the hospital in a bad way. He had no knowledge of what had pushed Tira over the edge or he might have thought twice about telling his older brother at all.

"I heard her. What happened?" Corrigan asked, jerking his head toward the room.

"I don't know," Simon said huskily. He leaned back against the wall beside his brother. His empty sleeve drew curious glances from a passerby, but he ignored it. "She saw me and started yelling." He broke off. His eyes were filled with torment. "I've never seen her like this."

"Nobody has," Corrigan said flatly. "I never figured a woman like Tira for a suicide."

Simon gaped at him. "A *what?*"

"What would you call combining alcohol and tran-

quilizers?'' Corrigan demanded. ''Good God, Mrs.
Lester said she had a loaded pistol in her hands!''

''A *pistol…?*'' Simon closed his eyes on a shudder
and ran a hand over his drawn face. He couldn't bear
to think about what might have happened. He was certain that he'd prompted her actions. He couldn't forget,
even now, the look on her face when he'd almost flatly
accused her of killing John. She hadn't said a word to
defend herself. She'd gone quiet; dangerously quiet. He
should never have left her alone. Worse, he should
never have said anything to her. He'd thought her a
strong, self-centered woman who wouldn't feel criti-
cism. Now, almost too late, he knew better.

''I went to see her yesterday,'' Simon confessed in
a haunted tone. ''She'd made some crazy remark at the
last cattle auction about trying to make me jealous. She
said she was only teasing, but it hit me the wrong way.
I told her that she wasn't the sort of woman I could be
jealous about. Then, yesterday, I told her how I felt
about her careless attitude toward the divorce only a
month after she married John, and letting him go off
to get himself killed on an oil rig.'' His broad shoulders
rose and fell defeatedly. ''I shouldn't have said it, but
I was angry that she'd tried to make me jealous, as if
she thought I might actually feel attracted to her.'' He
sighed. ''I thought she was so hard that nothing I said
would faze her.''

''And I thought I used to be blind,'' Corrigan said.

Simon glanced at him, scowling. ''What do you
mean?''

Corrigan looked at his brother and tried to speak.
Finally he just smiled faintly and turned away. ''Forget
it.''

The door to Tira's room opened a minute later and

Dr. Gaines came out. He spotted the two men down the hall and joined them.

"Don't go back in there," he told Simon flatly. "She's too close to the edge already. She doesn't need you to push her the rest of the way."

"I didn't do a damned thing," Simon shot back, and now he looked dangerous, "except walk in the door!"

Dr. Gaines' lips thinned. He glanced at Corrigan, who only shrugged and shook his head.

"I'm going to try to get her to go to a friend of mine, a therapist. She could use some counseling," Gaines added.

"She's not a nut case," Simon said, affronted.

Dr. Gaines looked into that cold, unaware face and frowned. "You were state attorney general for four years," he said. "You're still a well-known trial lawyer, an intelligent man. How can you be this stupid?"

"Will someone just tell me what's going on?" Simon demanded.

Dr. Gaines looked at Corrigan, who held out a hand, palm-up, inviting the doctor to do the dirty work.

"She'll kill us both if she finds out we told him," Gaines remarked to Corrigan.

"It's better than letting her die."

"Amen." He looked at Simon, who was torn between puzzlement and fury. "Simon, she's been in love with you for years," Dr. Gaines said in a hushed, reluctant tone. "I tried to get her to give up the ranch and all that fund-raising mania years ago, because they were only a way for her to keep near you. She wore herself out at it, hoping against hope that if you were in close contact, you might begin to feel something for her, but I knew that wasn't going to happen. All I had to do was see you together to realize she didn't have a chance. Am I right?" he asked Corrigan, who nodded.

Simon leaned back against the wall. He felt as if someone had put a knife right through him. He couldn't even speak.

"What you said to her was a kindness, although I don't imagine you see it that way now," Dr. Gaines continued doggedly. "She had to be made to see that she couldn't go on living a lie, and the changes in her life recently are proof that she's realized how you feel about her. She'll accept it, in time, and get on with her life. It will be the very best thing for her. She's trying to be all things to all people, until she was worn to a nub. She's been headed for a nervous breakdown for weeks, the way she's pushed herself, with this one-woman art show added to the load she was already carrying. But she'll be all right." He put a sympathetic hand on Simon's good arm. "It's not your fault. She's levelheaded about everything except you. But if you want to help her, for old time's sake, stay away from her. She's got enough on her plate right now."

He nodded politely to Corrigan and went on down the hall.

Simon still hadn't moved, or spoken. He was pale and drawn, half crazy from the doctor's revelation.

Corrigan got on the other side of him and took his arm, drawing him along. "We'll get a cup of coffee somewhere on the way back to your office," he told his older brother.

Simon allowed himself to be pulled out the door. He wasn't sure he remembered how to walk. He felt shattered.

Minutes later, he was sitting in a small café with his brother, drinking strong coffee.

"She tried to kill herself over me," Simon said finally.

"She missed. She won't try again. They'll make sure of it." He leaned forward. "Simon, she's been overextending for years, you know that. No one woman could have done as much as she has without risking her health, if not her sanity. If it hadn't been what you said to her, it would have been something else…maybe even this showing at the gallery that she was working night and day to get ready for."

Simon forced himself to breathe normally. He still couldn't quite believe it all. He sipped his coffee and stared into space.

"Did you know how she felt?" he asked Corrigan.

"She didn't tell me, if that's what you mean," his brother said. "But it was fairly obvious, the way she talked about you. I felt sorry for her. We all knew how much you loved Melia, that you've never let yourself get close to another woman since the wreck. Tira had to know that there was no hope in that direction."

The coffee in Simon's cup sloshed a little as he put it down. "It seems so clear now," he remarked absently. "She was always around, even when there didn't seem a reason for it. She worked on committees for organizations I belonged to, she did charity work for businesses where I was a trustee." He shook his head. "But I never noticed."

"I know."

He looked up. "John knew," he said suddenly.

Corrigan hesitated. Then he nodded.

Simon sucked in a harsh breath. "Good God, I broke up their marriage!"

"Maybe. I don't know. Tira never talks about John." His eyes narrowed thoughtfully. "But haven't you ever noticed that she and John's father are still friends? He doesn't blame her for his son's death. Shouldn't he, if it was all Tira's fault?"

Simon didn't want to think about it. He was sick to his stomach. "I pushed her at John," he recalled.

"I remember. They seemed to have a lot in common."

"They had me in common." Simon laughed bitterly. "She loved *me*..." He took a long sip of coffee and burned his mouth. The pain was welcome; it took his mind off his conscience.

"She can't ever know that we told you that," Corrigan said firmly, looking as formidable as his brother. "She's entitled to salvage a little of her pride. The newspapers got hold of the story, Simon. It's in the morning edition. The headline's really something—local socialite in suicide attempt. She's going to have hell living it down. I don't imagine they'll let her see a newspaper, but someone will tell her, just the same." His voice was harsh. "Some people love rubbing salt in wounds."

Simon rested his forehead against his one hand. He was so drained that he could barely function. It had been the worst day of his life; in some ways, worse than the wreck that had cost him everything.

For years, Tira's eyes had warmed at his approach, her mouth had smiled her welcome. She'd become radiant just because he was near her, and he hadn't known how she felt, with all those blatant signs.

Now, this morning, she'd looked at him with such hatred that he still felt sick from the violence of it. Her eyes had flashed fire, her face had burned with rage. He'd never seen her like that.

Corrigan searched his brother's worn face. "Don't take it so hard, Simon. None of this is your fault. She put too much pressure on herself and now she's paying the consequences. She'll be all right."

"She loved me," he said again, speaking the words harshly, as if he still couldn't believe them.

"You can't make people love you back," his brother replied. "Funny, Dorie and I saw her in the grocery store a few weeks ago, and she said that same thing. She had no illusions about the way you felt, regardless of how it looks."

Simon's eyes burned with anguish. "You don't know what I said to her, though. I accused her of killing John, of being so unconcerned about his happiness that she let him go into a dangerous job that he didn't have the experience to handle." His face twisted. "I said that she was shallow and cold and selfish, that I had nothing but contempt for her and that I'd never let a woman like her get close to me..." His eyes closed. "Dear God, how it must have hurt her to hear that from me."

Corrigan let out a savage breath. "Why didn't you just load the gun for her?"

"Didn't I?" the older man asked with tortured eyes.

Corrigan backed off. "Well, it's water under the bridge now. She's safely out of your life and she'll learn to get along on her own, with a little help. You can go back to your law practice and consider yourself off the endangered species list."

Simon didn't say another word. He stared into his coffee with sightless eyes until it grew cold.

* * *

Tira slept for the rest of the day. When she opened her eyes, the room was empty. There was a faint light from the wall and she felt pleasantly drowsy.

The night nurse came in, smiling, to check her vital signs. She was given another dose of medicine. Minutes later, without having dared remember the state she was in that morning, she went back to sleep.

When she woke up, a tall, blond, handsome man with dark eyes was sitting by the bed, looking quite devastating in white slacks and a red pullover knit shirt.

"Charles," she mumbled, and smiled. "How nice of you to come!"

"Who'll I talk to if you kill yourself, you idiot?" he muttered, glowering at her. "What a stupid thing to do."

She pushed herself up on an elbow, and pushed the mass of red-gold hair out of her eyes. She made a rough sound in her throat. "I wasn't trying to commit suicide!" she grumbled. "I got drunk and Mrs. Lester found an old empty prescription bottle and went ballistic." She shifted sleepily and yawned. "Well, I can't blame her, I guess. I still had the pistol in my hand and there was a hole in the wall…"

"Pistol!?"

"Calm down," she said, grimacing. "My head hurts. Yes, a pistol." She grinned at him a little sheepishly. "I was going to shoot the mouse."

His eyes widened. "Excuse me?"

"There's a mouse," she said. "I've set traps and put out bait, and he just keeps coming back into my kitchen. After a couple of drinks, I remembered a scene in *True Grit*, where John Wayne shot a rat, and when I got halfway through the whiskey bottle, it seemed perfectly logical that I should do that to my mouse."

She chuckled a little weakly. "You had to be there," she added helplessly.

"I suppose so." He searched her bloodshot eyes. "All those charity events, anybody calls and asks you to help, and you work day and night to organize things. You're everybody's helper. Now you're working on a collection of sculpture and still trying to keep up with your social obligations. I'm surprised you didn't fall out weeks ago. I tried to tell you. You know I did."

She nodded and sighed. "I know. I just didn't realize how hard I was working."

"You never do. You need to get married and have kids. That would keep you busy."

She lifted both eyebrows. "Are you offering to sacrifice yourself?"

He chuckled. "Maybe it would be the best thing for both of us," he said wistfully. "We're in love with people who don't want us. At least we like each other."

"Yes. But marriage should be more than that."

He shrugged. "Just a thought." He leaned over and patted her hand. "Get well. There's a society ball next week and you have to go with me. She's going to be there."

Tira knew who *she* was—his sister-in-law, the woman that Percy would have died to marry. She'd never noticed him, despite his blazing good looks, before she married his half brother. In fact, she seemed to actually dislike him, and Charles's half brother was twenty years her senior, a stiff-necked stuffed-shirt whom nobody in their circle had any use for. The marriage was a complete mystery.

"I don't have a dress."

"Buy one," he instructed.

She hesitated.

"I'll protect you from him," he said after a minute, having realized that Simon would most likely be in attendance. "I swear on my glorious red Mark VIII that I won't leave your side for an instant all evening."

She gave him a wary glance. His mania about that car was well-known. He wouldn't even entrust it to a car wash. He washed and waxed it lovingly, inch by inch, and called it "Big Red."

"Well, if you're willing to swear on your car," she agreed.

He grinned. "You can ride in it."

"I'm honored!"

"I brought you some flowers," he added. "One of the nurses volunteered to put them in a vase for you."

She gave him a cursory appraisal and smiled. "The way you look, I'm not surprised. Women fall over each other to get to you."

"Not the one I wanted," he said sadly. "And now it's too late."

She slid her hand into his and pressed it gently. "I'm sorry."

"So am I." He shrugged. "Isn't it a damned shame? I mean, look what they're missing!"

She knew he was talking about Simon and the woman Charles wanted, and she grinned in spite of herself. "It's their loss. I'd love to go to the ball with you. He'll let me out of here today. Like to take me home?"

"Sure!"

But when the doctor came into the room, he was reluctant to let her leave.

She was sitting on the side of the bed. She gave him

a long, wise look. "I wasn't lying," she said. "Suicide was the very last thing from my mind."

"With a loaded pistol, which had been fired."

She pursed her lips. "Didn't anyone notice where the shot landed? At a round hole in the baseboard?"

He frowned.

"The mouse!" she said. "I've been after him for weeks! Don't you watch old John Wayne movies? It was in *True Grit!*"

All at once, realization dawned in his eyes. "The rat writ."

"Exactly!"

He burst out laughing. "You were going to shoot the mouse?"

"I'm a good shot," she protested. "Well, when I'm sober. I won't miss him next time!"

"Get a trap."

"He's too wily," she protested. "I've tried traps and baits."

"Buy a cat."

"I'm allergic to fur," she confessed miserably.

"How about those electronic things you plug into the wall?"

She shook her head. "Tried it. He bit the electrical cord in half."

"Didn't it kill him?"

Her eyebrows arched. "No. Actually he seemed even healthier afterward. I'll bet he'd enjoy arsenic. Nope, I have to shoot him."

The doctor and Charles looked at each other. Then they both chuckled.

The doctor did see her alone later, for a few minutes while Charles was bringing the car around to the hospital entrance. "Just one more thing," he said gently.

"Regardless of what Simon said, you didn't kill John. Nobody, no woman, could have stopped what happened. He should never have married you in the first place."

"Simon kept throwing us together," she said. "He thought we made the perfect couple," she added bitterly.

"Simon never knew," he said. "I'm sure John didn't tell him, and you kept your own silence."

She averted her eyes. "John was the best friend Simon had in the world. If he'd wanted Simon to know, he'd have told him. That being the case, I never felt that I had the right." She looked at him. "I still don't. And you're not to tell him, either. He deserves to have a few unshattered illusions. His life hasn't been a bed of roses so far. He's missing an arm, and he's still mourning Melia."

"God knows why," Dr. Gaines added, because he'd known all about the elegant Mrs. Hart, things that even Tira didn't know.

"He loved her," she said simply. "There's no accounting for taste, is there?"

He smiled gently. "I guess not."

"You know, you really are a nice man, Dr. Gaines," she added.

He chuckled. "That's what my wife says all the time."

"She's right," she agreed.

"Don't you have family?"

She shook her head. "My father died of a heart attack, and my mother died even before he did. She had cancer. It was hard to watch, especially for Dad. He loved her too much."

"You can't love people too much."

She looked up at him with such sadness that her face seemed to radiate it. "Yes, you can," she said solemnly. "But I'm going to learn how to stop."

Charles pulled up at the curb and Dr. Gaines waved them off.

"Look at him," Charles said with a grin. "He's drooling! He wants my car." He stepped down on the accelerator. "Everybody wants my car. But it's mine. Mine!"

"Charles, you're getting obsessed with this automobile," she cautioned.

"I am not!" He glanced at her. "Careful, you'll get fingerprints on the window. And I do hope you wiped your shoes before you got in."

She didn't know whether to laugh or cry.

"I'm kidding!" he exclaimed.

She let out a sigh of relief. "And Dr. Gaines wanted *me* to have therapy," she murmured.

He threw her a glare. "I do not need therapy. Men love their cars. One guy even wrote a song about how much he loved his truck."

She glanced around the luxurious interior of the pretty car, leather coated with a wood-grained dash, and nodded. "Well, I could love Big Red," she had to confess. She leaned back against the padded headrest and closed her eyes.

He patted the dash. "Hear that, guy? You're getting to her!"

She opened one eye. "I'm calling the therapist the minute we get to my house."

He lifted both blond eyebrows. "Does he like cars?"

"I give up!"

* * *

When she arrived home, she was met at the door by a hovering, worried Mrs. Lester.

"It was an old, empty prescription bottle!" Tira told the kindly older woman. "And the pistol wasn't for me, it was for that mouse we can't catch in the kitchen!"

"The mouse?"

"Well, we can't trap him or drive him out, can we?" she queried.

The housekeeper blushed all the way to her white hairline and wrung her hands in the apron. "It was the way it looked..."

Tira went forward and hugged her. "You're a doll and I love you. But I was only drunk."

"You never drink," Mrs. Lester stated.

"I was driven to it," she replied.

Mrs. Lester looked at Charles. "By him?" she asked with a twinkle in her dark eyes. "You shouldn't let him hang around here so much, if he's driving you to drink."

"See?" he murmured, leaning down. "She wants my car, that's why she wants me to leave. She can't stand having to look at it day after day. She's obsessed with jealousy, eaten up with envy..."

"What's he talking about?" Mrs. Lester asked curiously.

"He thinks you want his car."

Mrs. Lester scoffed. "That long red fast flashy thing?" She sniffed. "Imagine me, riding around in something like that!"

Charles grinned. "Want to?" he asked, raising and lowering his eyebrows.

She chuckled. "You bet I do! But I'm much too old for sports cars, dear. Tira's just right."

"Yes, she is. And she needs coddling."

"I'll fatten her up and see that she gets her rest. I knew I should never have let her talk me into that vacation. The first time I leave her in a month, and look what happens! And the newspapers...!" She stopped so suddenly that she almost bit her tongue through.

Tira froze in place. "What newspapers?"

Mrs. Lester made a face and exchanged a helpless glance with Charles.

"You, uh, made the headlines," he said reluctantly.

She groaned. "Oh, for heaven's sake, there goes my one-woman show!"

"No, it doesn't," Charles replied. "I spoke to Bob this morning before I came after you. He said that the phone's rung off the hook all morning with queries about the show. He figures you'll make a fortune from the publicity."

"I don't need..."

"Yes, but the outreach program does," he reminded her. He grinned. "They'll be able to buy a new van!"

She smiled, but her heart wasn't in it. She didn't want to be notorious, whether or not she deserved to.

"Cheer up," he said. "It'll be old news tomorrow. Just don't answer the phone for a day or two. It will blow over as soon as some new tragedy catches the editorial eye."

"I guess you're right."

"Next Saturday," he reminded her. "I'll pick you up at six."

"Where will you be until then?" she asked, surprised, because he often came by for coffee in the afternoon.

"Memphis," he said with a sigh. "A business deal

that I have to conduct personally. I'll be out of town for a week. Bad timing, too."

"I'll be fine," she assured him. "Mrs. Lester's right here."

"I guess so. I do worry about you." He smiled sheepishly. "I don't have any family, either. You're sort of the only relative I have, even though you aren't."

"Same here."

He searched her eyes. "Two of a kind, aren't we? We loved not wisely, and too well."

"As you said, it's their loss," she said stubbornly. "Have a safe trip. Are you taking Big Red?"

He shook his head. "They won't let me take him on the plane," he said. "Walters is going to stand guard over him in the garage with a shotgun while I'm gone, though. Maybe he won't pine."

She burst out laughing. "I'm glad I have you for a friend," she said sincerely.

He took her hand and held it gently. "That works both ways. Take care. I'll phone you sometime during the week, just to make sure you're okay. If you need me…"

"I have your mobile number," she assured him. "But I'll be fine."

"See you next week, then."

"Thanks for the ride home," she said.

He shrugged and flashed her a white smile. "My pleasure."

She watched him drive away with sad eyes. She was going to have to live down the bad publicity without telling her side of the story. Well, what did it matter, she reasoned. It could, after all, have been worse.

Three

The week passed slowly until the charity ball on Saturday evening. It was to be a lavish one, hosted by the Carlisles, a founding family in the area and large supporters of the local hospital's charity work. Their huge brick mansion was just south of the perimeter of San Antonio, set in a grove of mesquite and pecan trees with its own duck pond and a huge formal garden. Tira had always loved coming to the house in the past for these gatherings, but she knew that Simon would be on the guest list. It was going to be hard facing him again after what had happened. It was going to be difficult appearing in public at all.

She did plan to go down with all flags flying, however, having poured her exquisite figure into a sleeveless, long black velvet evening gown with lace appliqués in entrancing places and a lace-up bodice that left little gaps from her diaphragm to her breasts. Her hair was in an elegant French twist with a diamond clip that matched her dangling earrings and delicate waterfall diamond necklace. She looked wealthy and sophisticated and Charles gave her a wicked grin when she came through to the living room with a black velvet and jewel wrap over one bare shoulder. It was November and the weather was unseasonably warm, so the wrap was just right.

Charles dressed up nicely, she thought, studying him. His tuxedo played up his extreme good looks and his fairness.

"Don't we make a pair?" he mused, glancing in the hall mirror at them. "Pity it isn't the right one."

"We'll both survive the evening," she assured him.

"Only if we drink hard enough," he said with graveyard humor. Then he noticed her expression and grimaced. "Sorry," he said genuinely.

"No need to apologize," she replied with a wry smile. "I did something stupid and had the misfortune to be found doing it. I'll survive all the gossip. But whatever you do, don't leave me alone with Simon, okay?"

"Count on it. What are friends for?"

She smiled at him. "To get us through rough times," she said, and was suddenly very grateful that she had a friend as good as Charles.

Charles chided her gently for her growing and obvious nervousness as he drove rapidly down the road that led to the Carlisle estate. "Don't worry so. You're old news," he reminded her. "There's the local political scandal to latch onto now."

"What political scandal?" she asked. "And how do you know about it when you've been out of town?"

"Because our lieutenant governor has been participating in a conference on the problems of inner cities in Memphis. I sat next to him on the flight home," he said smugly. Keeping his eyes on the road, he leaned toward her. "It seems that the attorney general intervened in a criminal case for a friend. The criminal he got paroled was serving time for armed robbery, but when he got out, he went right home and killed his ex-wife for testifying against him and is now back in prison. But the wheels of political change are going to roll over the governor's fair-haired boy."

"Oh, my goodness," she burst out. "But he was only doing a kindness. How could he know...?"

"He couldn't, and he isn't really to blame, but the opposition party is going to use it to crucify him. I understand his resignation is forthcoming momentarily."

"What a shame," Tira said honestly. "He's done a wonderful job. I met him at one of the charity benefits earlier this year and thought how lucky we were to have elected someone so capable to the position! Now, if he resigns, I guess the governor will have to temporarily appoint someone to finish his term."

"No doubt he will."

"Maybe he'll slide out of it. Lots of politicians do."

"Not this time, I'm afraid," Charles said. "He's made some bitter enemies since he took office. They'll love the opportunity to settle the score."

She recalled that Simon had antagonized plenty of people when he held the office of state attorney general. But it would have taken more than a scandal to unseat him. He had a clever habit of turning weapons against their wielders.

She closed her eyes and ground her teeth as she realized how pitiful she was about him, still. Everything reminded her of Simon. She hadn't wanted to come tonight, either, but the alternative was to stay home and let the whole city know what a coward she was. She had to hold her head up high and pretend that everything was fine, when her whole world was lying in shards around her feet.

She hadn't tried to kill herself, but one particularly lurid newspaper account said she had, and added that it had been over former attorney general Simon Hart, who'd rejected her. It was in a newspaper published by a relative of Jill Sinclair, a woman who'd been a rival of Tira's for Simon during the past few years. Tira had been even more humiliated at that particular story, but when she'd phoned the reporter who wrote it, he denied any knowledge of Jill Sinclair. Still, she was certain dear Jill had a hand in it.

Tira shuddered, realizing that Simon must have seen the story, too. He'd know what a fool she'd been over him, which was just one more humiliation. Living that down wasn't going to be easy. But she did have Charles beside her. And he had his own ordeal to face, because his sister-in-law would certainly be present.

A valet came to park the car for Charles, who was torn between escorting Tira inside or accompanying the elegantly dressed young man assigned to the car placement to make sure he didn't put a scratch on "Big Red."

"Go ahead," Tira said with amused resignation. "I'll wait on the steps for you."

"You're such a doll," he murmured and made a kissing motion toward her. "How many women in the world would understand a man's passion for his car?

Here, son, I'll just ride down with you to the parking lot.''

The valet seemed torn between shock and indignation.

"He's in love with it!" Tira called to the young man. "He can't help himself. Just humor him!"

The valet broke into a wide grin and climbed under the steering wheel.

It was unfortunate that while she was waiting on the wide porch for Charles to return, Simon and his date got out of his elegant Town Car at the steps and let the valet drive it off. He looked devastating, as usual. He was wearing the prosthesis, she noticed, and wondered at how much he seemed to use it these days. Just after the wreck, he wouldn't be caught dead wearing an artificial arm.

The woman with him was Jill Sinclair herself, a socialite, twice divorced and wealthy, with short black hair and dark eyes and a figure that drew plenty of interest. It would, Tira thought wickedly, considering that her red sequined dress must have been sprayed on and the paint ran out at midthigh. Advertising must pay, she mused, because Simon certainly seemed pleased as he smiled down at the small woman and held her elbow as they climbed up the steps.

He didn't see Tira until they were almost at the top. When he did, he seemed to jerk, as if the sight of her was unexpected.

She didn't let anything of her feelings show, despite the pain of seeing him now when her whole life had been laid bare in the press. She did her best not to let her embarrassment show, either. She smiled carelessly and nodded politely at the couple and deliberately turned away in the direction where Charles and the valet were just coming into view.

"Why, how brave she is," Jill Sinclair purred to Simon, just loud enough for Tira to hear her. "I'd never have had the nerve to face all these people after that humiliating story in the—Simon!"

Her voice died completely. Tira didn't look toward them. Her face was flaming and she knew her accelerated heartbeat was making her shake visibly. She and Jill had never liked each other, but the woman seemed to be looking for a way to hurt her. She was obviously exuding her power since she'd finally managed to get Simon to notice her and take her out. God knew, she'd been after him for years. Tira's fall from grace had obviously benefitted her.

Charles bounded up the steps and took Tira's arm. "Sorry about that," he said sheepishly.

"You love your car," she replied with a warm smile. "I understand."

"You're one in a million," he mused. His hand fell to grasp hers, and when she looked inside the open doors she knew why. His half brother was there, and so was his sister-in-law, looking unhappy.

"Gene," he called to his older half brother. "Nice to see you." He shook the other man's hand. Gene was tall and severe-looking with thinning gray hair. The woman beside him was tiny and blond and lovely, but she had the most tragic brown eyes Tira had ever seen.

"Hello, Nessa," Charles said to the woman, his face guarded, a polite smile on his lips.

"Hello, Charles, Tira," Nessa replied in her soft, sweet voice. "You both look very nice. Isn't this a good turnout?" she added nervously. "They'll make a lot of money at five hundred dollars a couple."

"Yes," Tira agreed with a broad smile. "The hospital outreach program will probably be able to afford two vans and the services of another nurse!"

"For indigents," Gene Marlowe said huffily, "who won't pay a penny of their own health care."

The other three people looked at him as if he'd gone mad. He glared at them, reddening. "I have to see Todd Groves about a contract we're pursuing. If you'll excuse me? Nessa, don't just stand there! Come along."

Nessa ground her teeth together as Gene took her arm roughly. Charles looked as if he might attack his own brother right there. Tira caught his hand and tugged.

"I'm starving," she told him quickly, exchanging speaking glances with a suddenly relieved Nessa. "Feed me!"

Charles hesitated for an instant, during which Gene dragged Nessa away toward a group of men.

"Damn him!" Charles bit off, his normally pleasant face contorted and threatening.

Tira shook his hand gently. "You're broadcasting," she murmured, bumping deliberately against his side to distract him. "Come on, before you cause her any more trouble than she's already got."

He let out a weary sigh. "Why did she marry him?" he groaned. *"Why?"*

"Whatever the reason doesn't matter much now. Let's go."

She pulled until he let her lead him to the long buffet table, where expensive nibbles and champagne were elegantly arranged.

"This is going to eat up all the profits," Tira murmured worriedly, noting the crystal flutes that were provided for the champagne, and the fact that caviar was furnished as well.

Charles leaned toward her. "It's grocery store caviar, and the champagne is the sort they deliver in big round metal tractor trucks…"

"Charles!" She couldn't repress a giggle at the insinuation, and just as she felt her face going red from glee, she looked up and saw Simon's pale eyes glittering at her from across the room. She averted her eyes to the table and didn't look in that direction again. His expression had been far different from the one he'd worn when he'd seen her in the hospital. Now it was indignant and outraged, as if he blamed her for the publicity that made him look guilty, too.

Charles did waltz divinely. Tira found herself on the floor with him time after time. People noticed her, and there were some obvious whispers, which probably concerned her "suicide attempt." She was uncomfortable at first, but then she realized that the opinion of most of these people didn't matter to her. She knew the truth about what had happened and so did Charles. If the others wanted to believe her to be so weak and helpless that she'd die rather than face up to her failures, let them.

"Doesn't it worry you, being seen with such a notorious woman?" she chided when they were standing again at the buffet table with more champagne.

"Notorious women are fascinating," he returned, and smiled. His eyes lifted to his half brother and Nessa and his jaw clenched. The two of them were going out the door and Nessa looked as if she were crying.

"You can't," she said, catching his arm when he looked as if he might follow them.

"She should leave him."

"She'll have to make that decision for herself."

He glanced down at her with worried eyes. "She isn't like you. She isn't independent and spirited. She's shy and gentle and people take advantage of her."

"And you want to protect her. I understand. But you can't, not tonight."

He made a rough sound in his throat. "Damn it!"

She leaned against him affectionately for an instant. "I'm sorry. I really am."

His arm slipped around her shoulders. "One day," he promised himself.

She nodded. "One day."

"Why, Charles, how handsome you look!" Jill Sinclair's high-pitched, grating voice turned them around. "Are you enjoying yourself?"

"I'm having a great time," Charles said through his teeth. "How about you?"

"Oh, Simon is just the most wonderful escort," she sighed and glanced at Tira with half-closed eyes. "We've been everywhere together lately. There are *so* many charity dos this time of year. And how are you, Tira? I was so sorry to hear about your near tragedy!" She was almost purring, enjoying Tira's stiff posture and cold face. She raised her voice, drawing attention from the couples hovering near the buffet table. "Isn't it a pity that the newspapers made such a big thing of your suicide attempt? I mean, the humiliation of having your feelings made public must be awful. And for the gossips to say that you wanted to die just because Simon couldn't love you back...why he was just shattered that you made him look like a coldhearted villain in the eyes of his friends. God knows, it isn't his fault that he doesn't love you!"

Tira was too shaken by the unexpected attack to reply. Charles wasn't.

"Why, you prissy little cat," Charles said with cold venom, making Jill actually catch her breath in surprise at the unexpected verbal jab. "Why don't you go sharpen your claws on the curtains?"

He took Tira's arm and led her away. She was so shocked and outraged that she couldn't even manage words. She wanted to empty the punch bowl over the woman, but that was hardly the sort of thing to do at a benefit ball. Her proud spirit had all but been broken by recent events. She was still licking her wounds.

Simon was talking to a man near the door that Charles was urging her toward. He paused in midsentence and looked at Tira's white face with curious concern.

Before he could speak, Charles did. "Never mind adding your two cents worth. Your girlfriend said it all for you."

Charles prodded her forward and Tira didn't look Simon's way. She was barely able to see where she was going at all. Until Jill's piece of mischief, she'd actually thought she could get through the evening unscathed.

"That cat!" Charles muttered as they made their way to the bottom of the steps.

"The world is full of them," she breathed. "And how they love to claw you when you're down!"

None of the valets were anywhere in sight. Charles grumbled. "I'll have to go fetch the car. Stay right here. Will you be all right?"

"I'm fine, now that we're outside," she said.

He gave her a last, worried glance, and went around the house to the parking area.

She drew her wrap closer, because the air was chilly. Once, she'd have made Jill pay dearly for her nasty comments, but not anymore. Now, her proud spirit was dulled and she'd actually walked away from a fight. It wasn't like her. Charles obviously knew that, or he wouldn't have rushed her out the door so quickly.

She heard footsteps behind her and her heart jumped, because she knew the very sound of Simon's feet. Her eyes closed as she wished him in China—anywhere but here!

"What did she say to you?" he asked shortly.

She wouldn't turn; she wouldn't look at him. She couldn't bear to look at him. The humiliation of having him know how she felt about him was so horrible that it suffocated her. All those years of hiding it from him, cocooning her love in secrecy. And now he knew, the whole world knew. And worst of all, she loved him still. Just being near him was agony.

"I said, what did she say to you?" he repeated, moving directly in front of her so that she had to look at him.

She lifted her eyes to his black tie and no further. Her voice was choked, and stiff with wounded pride. "Go and ask her."

There was a rough sigh and she saw his good hand go irritably into the pocket of his trousers. "This isn't like you," he said after a minute. "You don't run and you don't cry, regardless of what people say to you. You fight back. Why are you leaving?"

She lifted tired eyes to his and hated the sudden jolt of her heart at the sight of his beloved face. She clenched every muscle in her body to keep from sobbing out her rage and hurt. "I don't care what anyone thinks of me," she said huskily, "least of all your malicious girlfriend. Yes, I've spent most of my life fighting, one way or another, but I'm tired. I'm tired of everything.''

Her lack of animation disturbed him, along with the defeat in her voice, the cool poise. "You can't be worried about what the newspapers said," he said, his voice deep and slow and oddly tender.

"Can't I? Why not? They believed every word." She inclined her head toward the ballroom.

His features were unusually solemn. "I know you better than they do."

She searched his pale eyes in the dim light from the house. Her heart clenched. "You don't know me at all, Simon," she said with painful realization. "You never did."

He seemed to stiffen. "I thought I did. Until you divorced John."

Her heart stilled at the reference. "And until he died." Defeat was in every line of her elegant body. "Yes, I know, I'm a murderess."

His face went taut. "I didn't say that!"

"You might as well have!" she shot back, raising her voice, not caring if the whole world heard her. "If Melia had died in a similar manner, I'd never have believed you guilty of her death! I'd have known you well enough to be certain that you had no part in anything that would cause another human being harm. But then, I had a mad infatuation for you that I couldn't cure." She saw his sudden stillness. "Don't pretend that you didn't read all about it in the paper, Simon. Yes, it's true, why shouldn't I admit it? I was obsessed with you, desperate to be with you, in any way that I could. It didn't even matter that you only tolerated me. I could have lived on crumbs for the rest of my life—"

Her voice broke. She shifted on trembling legs and laughed with pure self-contempt. "What a fool I was! What a silly fool. I'm twenty-eight years old and I've only just realized how stupid I am!"

He frowned. "Tira…"

She moved back a step, her green eyes blazing with ruptured pride. "Jill told me what you said, that you blame me for making you look like a villain in public with my so-called suicide attempt, as well as for John's death. Well, go ahead, hate me! I don't give a damn anymore!" she spat, out of control and not caring. "I'm not even surprised to see you with Jill, Simon. She's as opinionated and narrow-minded as you are, and she knows how to put the knife in, too. I daresay you're a match made in heaven!"

His face clenched visibly. "And you don't care that I'm with another woman tonight, instead of with you?" he chided, hitting back as hard as he could, with a mocking smile on his lips.

Her face went absolutely white. But if it killed her, he'd never hear from her how she did care. She smiled deliberately. "No," she agreed softly. "Actually I don't. All this notoriety accomplished one good thing. It made me see how I'd wasted the past few miserable years mooning over you! You did me a favor when you told me what you really thought of me. I'm free of you at last, Simon," she lied with deliberation. "And I've never been quite so happy in all my life!"

And with that parting shot, she turned and walked slowly to the driveway where Charles was pulling up in front of the house, leaving Simon rigidly in place with an expression of shock that delighted her wounded pride.

After what she'd said, she didn't expect Simon to

follow her, and he didn't. When Charles had installed her in the passenger seat, she caught just a glimpse of Simon's straight back rapidly returning to the house. She even knew the posture. He was furious. Good! Let him be furious. She was not going to care. She wasn't!

"Take it easy," Charles said softly. "You'll burst something."

"I know how you felt earlier," she returned, leaning her hot forehead against the glass of the window. "Damn him! And damn her, too!"

"What did he say to you?"

"He wanted to know what she said, and then he gave me his opinion of my character again. But this time, he didn't know he'd hit me where it hurt. I made sure of it."

Charles let out a long breath. "Why can't we love to order?" he asked philosophically.

"I don't know. If you ever find out, you can tell me." She stared out the dark window at the flat landscape passing by. Her heart felt as if it might break all over again.

"He's an idiot."

"So is Jill. So is Gene. We're all idiots. Maybe we're certifiable and we can become a circus act."

They drove in silence until they reached her house. He turned off the engine and stared at her worriedly. She was pale and she looked so miserable that he hurt for her.

"Go inside and change your clothes and pack a suitcase," he said suddenly.

"What?"

"We'll fly down to Nassau for a long weekend. It's just Saturday. We'll take a three-day vacation. I have a friend who owns a villa there. He and his wife love company. We'll eat conch chowder and play at the casino and lay on the beach. How about it?''

She brightened. "Could we?"

"We could. You need a break and so do I. Be a gambler."

It sounded like fun. She hadn't been happy in such a long time. "Okay," she said.

"Okay." He grinned. "Maybe we'll cheer up in foreign parts. Don't take too long. I'll run home and change and make a few phone calls. I should be back within an hour."

"Great!"

It was great. The brief holiday made Tira feel as if she had a new lease on life. Charles was wonderful, undemanding company, much more like a beloved brother than a boyfriend. They padded all over Nassau, down West Bay Street to the docks and out on the pier to look at the ships in port, and all the way to the shopping district and the vast straw markets. Nassau was the most exciting, cosmopolitan city in the world to Tira. She never tired of going there. Just now, it was a godsend. She hated the memory of Jill's taunting words and Simon's angry accusations. It was good to have a breathing space from them, and the publicity.

They stretched their stay to five days instead of three and returned to San Antonio refreshed and rested, although Charles had confessed that he did miss his car. He proved it by rushing home as soon as the limousine he'd hired to meet them at the airport delivered Tira at her house.

"I'll phone you in the morning. We might have a game of tennis Saturday, if you're up to it," he said.

"I will be. Thanks, Charles. Thanks so much!"

He chuckled. "I enjoyed it. So long."

She watched the limousine pull away and walked slowly up to her front door. She hated homecomings. She had nothing here but Mrs. Lester and an otherwise empty house, and her work. It was cold compensation.

Mrs. Lester greeted her with enthusiasm. "I'm so glad you're home!" she said. "The phone rang off the hook the day after you left and didn't stop until three days ago." She shook her head. "I can't imagine why those newspaper people wanted to drag the whole subject up again, but I guess the shooting downtown Tuesday afternoon gave them something new to go after."

"What shooting?"

"Well, that man the attorney general had paroled— you remember?—was in court to be arraigned and he went right over the table toward the judge and almost killed him. They managed to pull him away and he grabbed the bailiff's gun. They had to shoot him! It's been on all the television stations. They had the most awful photographs of it!"

Tira actually gasped. "For heaven's sake!"

"Mr. Hart was right in the middle of it, too. He had a case and was waiting for it to be called when the prisoner got loose."

"Simon? Was he…hurt?" Tira had to ask.

"No. He was the one who pulled the man off the judge. The man had that bailiff's gun leveled right at him, they said, when a deputy sheriff shot the man. It was a close call for Mr. Hart. A real close call. But you'd never think it worried him to hear him talk on television. He was as cold as ice."

She sat down on the edge of the sofa and thanked God for Simon's life. She wished that they were still friends, even distant ones, so that she could phone him and tell him so. But there was a wall between them now.

"Mr. Hart wondered why you hadn't gotten in touch with him, afterward," Mrs. Lester said, hesitating.

Tira glanced at her breathlessly. "He called?"

She nodded and then grimaced. "He wanted to know if you heard about the shooting and if you'd been concerned. I had to tell him that you were away, and didn't know a thing, and when he asked where, he got that out of me, too. I hope it was all right that I told him."

Simon would think she went on a lover's holiday with Charles. Well, why shouldn't he? He believed she was a murderess and a flighty, shallow flirt and suicidal. Let him think whatever else he liked. She couldn't be any worse in his eyes than she already was.

"Give a dog a bad name," she murmured.

"What?" Mrs. Lester asked.

She dragged her mind back to the subject at hand. "Yes, of course, it's perfectly all right that you told him, Mrs. Lester," Tira said quietly. "I had a wonderful time in Nassau."

"Did you good, I expect, and Mr. Percy is a nice man."

"A very nice man," Tira agreed. She got to her feet. "I'm tired. I think I'll lie down for a while, so don't fix anything to eat for another hour or so, will you?"

"Certainly, dear. You just rest. I'll have some coffee and sandwiches ready when you want them."

Would she ever want them? Tira wondered as she went slowly toward her bedroom. She was empty and cold and sick at heart. But that seemed to be her normal condition. At least for now.

Four

It was raining the day Tira began taking her sculptures to Bob Henderson's "Illuminations" art gallery for her showing. She was so gloomy she hardly felt the mist on her face. Christmas was only two weeks away and she was miserable and lonely. Only months before, she'd have phoned Simon and asked him to meet her for lunch in town, or she'd have shown up at some committee meeting or benefit conference at which he was present, just to feed her hungry heart on the sight of him. Now, she had nothing. Only Charles and his infrequent, undemanding company. Charles was a sweetheart, but it was like having a brother over for coffee.

She carried the last box carefully in the back door, which Lillian Day, the gallery's manager was holding open for her.

"That's the last of them, Lillian," Tira told her,

smiling as she surveyed the cluttered storage room. She shook her head. "I can't believe I did all those myself."

"It's a lot of work," Lillian agreed, smiling back. She bent to open one of the boxes and frowned slightly at what was inside. "Did you mean to include this?" she asked, indicating a bust of Simon that was painfully lifelike.

Tira's face closed up. "Yes, I meant to," she said curtly. "I don't want it."

Lillian wisely didn't say another word. "I'll place it with the others, then. The catalogs have been printed and they're perfect, I checked them myself. Everything's ready, including the caterer for the snack buffet and the media coverage. We're doing a Christmas motif for the buffet."

Media coverage. Tira ground her teeth. The last thing in the world she wanted to see now was a reporter.

Lillian, sensitive to moods, glanced at her reassuringly. "Don't worry. These were handpicked, by me," she added. "They won't ask any embarrassing questions, and anything they write for print will be about the show. Period."

Tira relaxed. "What would I do without you?" she asked, and meant it.

Lillian grinned. "Don't even think about trying. We're very glad to have your exhibit here."

Tira had worried about Simon's reaction to the showing, since he was a partner in Bob Henderson's gallery. They hadn't spoken since before his close call in the courtroom and she half expected him to cancel her exhibit. But he hadn't. Perhaps Mrs. Lester had been mistaken and he hadn't been angry that Tira hadn't phoned to check on him. Just because she hadn't called, it didn't mean that she hadn't worried. She'd had a few sleepless nights thinking about what could have happened to him. Despite her best efforts, her feelings for him hadn't changed. She was just as much in love with him now as she had been. She was only better at concealing it.

The night of the exhibit arrived. She was all nerves, and she was secretly glad that Charles would be by her side. Not that she expected Simon to show up, with the media present. He wouldn't want to give them any more ammunition to embarrass him with. But Charles would be a comfort to her.

Fate stepped in, however, to rob her of his presence. Charles phoned at the last minute, audibly upset, to tell her he couldn't go with her to the show.

"I'm more sorry than I can tell you, but Gene's had a heart attack," he said curtly.

"Oh, Charles, I'm so sorry!"

"No need to be. You know there's no love lost between us. But he's my half brother, just the same, and there's no one else to look after him. Nessa is in shock herself. I can't let her cope alone."

"How is he?"

"Stabilized, for the moment. I'm on my way to the hospital. Nessa's with him and he's giving her hell, as usual, even flat on his back," he said curtly.

"If there's anything I can do…"

"Thanks for your support. I'm sorry you have to go on your own. But it's unlikely that Simon will be there, you know," he added gently. "Just stick close to Lillian. She'll look out for you."

She smiled to herself. "I know she will. Let me know how it goes."

"Of course I will. See you."

He hung up. She stared at the phone blankly as she replaced the receiver. She looked good, she reasoned. Her black dress was a straight sheath, ankle-length, with spaghetti straps and a diamond necklace and earrings to set it off. It was a perfect foil for her pale, flawless complexion and her red-gold hair, done in a complicated topknot with tendrils just brushing her neck. From her austere get up, she looked more like a widow in mourning than a woman looking forward to Christmas, and she felt insecure and nervous. It would be the first time she'd appeared alone in public since the scandal and she was still uncomfortable around most people.

Well, she comforted herself as she went outside and climbed into her Jaguar, at least she didn't have to add Simon to her other complications tonight.

The gallery was packed full of interested customers, some of whom had probably only come for curiosity's sake. It wasn't hard to discern people who could afford the four-figure price tags on the sculptures from those who couldn't. Tira pretended not to notice. She took a flute of expensive champagne and downed half of it before she went with Lillian to mingle with the guests.

It didn't help that the first two people she saw were Simon and Jill.

"Oh, God," she ground out through her teeth, only too aware of the reporters and their sudden interest in him. "Why did he have to come?!"

Lillian took her arm gently. "Don't let him know that it bothers you. Smile, girl! We'll get through this."

"Do you think so?"

She plastered a cool smile to her lips as Simon pulled Jill along with him and came to a halt just in front of the two women.

"Nice crowd," he told Tira, his eyes slowly going over her exquisite figure in the close-fitting dress with unusual interest.

"A few art fans and a lot of rubberneckers, hadn't you noticed?" Tira said, sipping more champagne. Her fingers trembled a little and she held the flute with both hands, something Simon's keen eyes picked up on at once.

"Nice of you to come by," Lillian said quietly.

He glanced at her. "It would have been noticeable if I hadn't, considering that I own half the gallery." His attention turned back to Tira and his silvery eyes narrowed. "All alone? Where's your fair-haired shadow?"

She knew he meant Charles. She smiled lazily. "He couldn't make it."

"On the first night of your first exhibition?" he chided.

She drew in a sharp breath. "His half brother had a heart attack, if you must know," she said through her teeth. "He's at the hospital."

Simon's eyes flickered strangely. "And you have to be here, instead of at his side. Pity."

"He doesn't need comforting. Nessa does."

Jill, dressed in red again with a sprig of holly secured with a diamond clip in her black hair, moved closer to Simon. "We just stopped in for a peek at your work," she said, almost purring as she looked up at the tall man beside her. "We're on our way to the opera."

Tira averted her eyes. She loved opera. Many times

in the past, Simon had escorted her during the season. It hurt to remember how she'd looked forward to those chaste evenings with him.

"I don't suppose you go anymore?" Simon asked coldly.

She shrugged. "Don't have time," she said tightly.

"I noticed. You couldn't even be bothered to phone and check on me when that lunatic went wild in the courtroom."

Tira wouldn't look at him. "You can't hurt someone who's steel right through," she said.

"And you were out of the country when it happened."

She lifted her eyes to his hard face. "Yes. I was in Nassau with Charles, having a lovely time!"

His eyes seemed to blaze up at her.

Before the confrontation could escalate, Lillian diplomatically got between them. "Have you had time to look around?" she asked Simon.

"Oh, we've seen most everything," Jill answered for him. "Even the bust of Simon that Tira did. I was surprised that she was willing to sell it," she added in an innocent tone. "I wouldn't part with something so personal, Simon being such an old friend and all. But I guess under the circumstances, it was too painful a reminder of…things, wasn't it, dear?" she asked Tira.

Tira's hand automatically drew back, with the remainder of the champagne, but before she could toss it, Simon caught her wrist with his good hand.

"No catfights," he said through his teeth. "Jill, wait for me at the door, will you?"

"If you say so. My, she does look violent, doesn't she?" Jill chided, but she walked away quickly just the same.

"Get a grip on yourself!" Simon shot at Tira under his breath. "Don't you see the reporters staring at you?"

"I don't give a damn about the reporters," she flashed at him. "If she comes near me again, I swear I'll empty the punch bowl over her vicious little head!"

He let go of her wrist and something kindled in his pale eyes as he looked at her animated face. "That's more like you," he said in a deep, soft tone.

Tira flushed, aware that Lillian was quietly deserting her, stranding her with Simon.

"Why did you come?" she asked furiously.

"So the gossips wouldn't have a field day speculating about why I didn't," he explained. "It wouldn't have done either of us much good, considering what's been in print already."

She lifted her face, staring at him with cold eyes at the reference to things she only wanted to forget. "You've done your duty," she said. "You might as well go. And take the Wicked Witch of the West with you," she added spitefully.

"Jealous?" he asked in a sensuous tone.

Her face hardened. "I once asked you the same question. You can give yourself the same answer that you gave me. Like hell I'm jealous!"

He was watching her curiously, his eyes acutely alive in a strangely taciturn face. "You've lost weight," he remarked. "And you look more like a widow than a celebrity tonight. Why wear black?"

"I've decided that you were right. I should have mourned my husband. So now I'm in mourning," she said icily and with an arctic smile. "I expect to be in mourning for him until I die, and I'll never look at a man again. Doesn't that make you happy?"

He frowned slightly. "Tira..."

"Tira!"

The sound of a familiar voice turned them both around. Harry Beck, Tira's father-in-law, came forward, smiling, to embrace Tira. He turned to shake Simon's hand. "Great to see you both!" he said enthusiastically. "Dollface, you've outdone yourself," he told Tira, nodding toward two nearby sculptures. "I always knew you were talented, but this is sheer genius!"

Simon looked puzzled by Harry's honest enthusiasm for Tira's work, by his lack of hostility. She'd killed his only son, didn't he care?

"I'm glad to see you, Simon," Harry added with a smile. "It's been a long time."

"Simon was just leaving. Weren't you?" Tira added meaningfully.

"Someone's motioning to you," Harry noted, indicating Lillian frantically waving from across the room.

"It's Lillian. Will you excuse me?" Tira asked, smiling at Harry. "I won't be a minute." Simon, she ignored entirely.

The two men watched her go.

"I'm glad to see her looking so much better," Harry said on a sigh, shoving his hands into his pockets. "I've been worried since she went to the hospital."

"Do you really care what happens to her?" Simon asked curiously.

Harry was surprised. "Why wouldn't I be? She was my daughter-in-law. I've always been fond of her."

"She divorced John a month after they married and let him go off to work on a drill rig in the ocean," Simon returned. "He died there."

Harry stared at him blankly. "But that wasn't her fault."

"Wasn't it?"

"Why are you so bitter?" Harry wanted to know. "For God's sake, you can't think she didn't try to change him? He should have told her the truth before he married her, not let her find it out that way!"

Simon was puzzled. "Find what out?"

Jill glared at Simon, but he made a motion for her to wait another minute and turned back to Harry. "Find what out?" he repeated curtly.

"That John was homosexual, of course," Harry said, puzzled.

The blood drained out of Simon's face. He stared down at the older man with dawning comprehension.

"She didn't tell you?" Harry asked gently. He sighed and shook his head. "That's like her, though. She wanted to preserve your illusions about John, even if it meant sacrificing your respect for her. She couldn't tell you, I guess. I can't blame her. If he'd only been able to accept what he was…but he couldn't. He tried so hard to be what he thought I wanted. And he never seemed to understand that I'd have loved him regardless of how he saw his place in the world."

Simon turned away, his eyes finding Tira across the room. She wouldn't meet his gaze. She turned her back. He felt the pain right through his body.

"Dear God!" he growled when he realized what he'd done.

"Don't look like that," Harry said gently. "John made his own choice. It was nobody's fault. Maybe it was mine. I should have seen that he was distraught and done something."

Simon let out a breath. He was sick right to his soul. What a fool he'd been.

"She should have told you," Harry was saying. "You're a grown man. You don't need to be protected from the truth. She was always like that, even with John, trying to protect him. She'd have gone on with the marriage if he hadn't insisted on a divorce."

"I thought…she got the divorce."

"He got it, in her name, and cited mental cruelty." He shrugged. "I don't think he considered how it might look to an outsider. It made things worse for him. He only did it to save her reputation. He thought it would hurt her publicly if he made it look like she was at fault." He glanced at Simon. "That was right after your wreck and she was trying to take care of you. He thought it might appear as if she was having an affair with you and he found out. It might have damaged both of you in the public eye."

His teeth clenched. "I never touched her."

"Neither did John," Harry murmured heavily. "He couldn't. He cried in my arms about it, just before he saw an attorney. He wanted to love her. He did, in his way. But it wasn't in a conventional way at all."

Simon pushed back a strand of dark, wavy hair that had fallen on his brow. He was sweating because the gallery was overheated.

"Are you all right?" Harry asked with concern.

"I'm fine." He wasn't. He'd never be all right again. He glanced toward Tira with anguish in every line of his face. But she wouldn't even look at him.

Jill, sensing some problem, came back to join him, sliding her hand into his arm. "Aren't you ready? We'll miss the curtain."

"I'm ready," he said. He looked down at her and

realized that here was one more strike against him. He was giving aid and comfort to Tira's worst enemy in the city. He'd done it deliberately, of course, to make her even more uncomfortable. But that was before he knew the whole truth. Now he felt guilty.

"Hello. I'm Jill Sinclair. Have we met?" she asked Harry, smiling.

"No, we haven't. I'm—"

"We have to go," Simon said abruptly. He didn't want to add any more weapons to Jill's already full arsenal by letting Harry tell her about John, too. "See you, Harry."

"Sure. Good night."

"Who was that?" Jill asked Simon as they went toward the door.

"An old friend. Just a minute. There's something I have to do."

"Simon...!"

"I won't be a minute," he promised, and caught one of the gallery's sales-people alone long enough to make a request. She seemed puzzled, but she agreed. He went back to Jill and escorted her out of the gallery, casting one last regretful look toward Tira, who was speaking to a group of socialites at the back of the gallery.

"Half the works are sold already," Jill murmured. "I guess she'll make a fortune."

"She's donating it all to charity," he replied absently.

"She can afford to. It will certainly help her image and, God knows, she needs that right now."

He glanced at her. "That isn't why."

She shrugged. "Whatever you say, darling. *Brrrr,* I'm cold! Christmas is week after next, too." She peered up at him. "I hope you got me something pretty."

"I wouldn't count on it. I probably won't be in town for Christmas," he said not quite truthfully.

She sighed. "Oh, well, I might go and spend the holidays with my aunt in Connecticut. I do love snow!"

She was welcome to all she could find of it, he thought. His heart already felt as if he were buried in snow and ice. He knew that Harry's revelation would keep him awake all night.

Tira watched Simon leave with Jill. She was glad he'd gone. Perhaps now she could enjoy her show.

Lillian was giving her strange looks and when Harry came to say goodbye, he looked rather odd, too.

"What's wrong?" she asked Harry.

He started to speak and thought better of it. Let Simon tell her what he wanted her to know. He was tired of talking about the past; it was too painful.

He smiled. "It's a great show, kiddo, you'll make a mint."

"Thanks, Harry. I had fun doing it. Keep in touch, won't you?"

He leaned forward and kissed her cheek. "You know I will. How's Charlie?"

"His brother-in-law had a heart attack. He's not doing well."

"I'm really sorry. Always liked Charlie. Still do."

"I'll tell him you asked about him," she promised.

He smiled at her. "You do that. Keep well."

"You, too."

By the end of the evening, Tira was calmer, despite the painful memory of her argument with Simon's and

Jill's catty remarks. She could just picture the two of them in Simon's lavish apartment, sprawled all over each other in an ardent tangle. It made her sick. Simon had never kissed her, never touched her in anything but an impersonal way. She'd lived like a religious recluse for part of her life and she had nothing to show for her reticence except a broken heart and shattered pride.

"What a great haul," Lillian enthused, breaking into her thoughts. "You sold three-forths of them. The rest we'll keep on display for a few weeks and see how they do."

"I'm delighted," Tira said, and meant it. "It's all going to benefit the outreach program at St. Mark's."

"They'll be very happy with it, I'm sure."

Tira was walking around the gallery with the manager. Most of the crowd had left and a few stragglers were making their way to the door. She noticed the bust of Simon had a Sold sign on it, and her heart jumped.

"Who bought it?" Tira asked curtly. "It wasn't Jill Sinclair, was it?"

"No," Lillian assured her. "I'm not sure who bought it, but I can check, if you like."

"No, that's not necessary," Tira said, clamping down hard on her curiosity. "I don't care who bought it. I only wanted it out of my sight. I don't care if I never see Simon Hart again!"

Lillian sighed worriedly, but she smiled when Tira glanced toward her and offered coffee.

Simon watched the late-night news broadcast from his easy chair, nursing a whiskey sour, his second in half an hour. He'd taken Jill home and adroitly avoided her coquettish invitation to stay the night. After what he'd learned from Harry Beck, he had to be by himself to think things out.

There was a brief mention of Tira's showing at the gallery and how much money had been raised for charity. He held his breath, but nothing was said about her suicide attempt. He only hoped the newspapers would be equally willing to put the matter aside.

He sipped his drink and remembered unwillingly all the horrible things he'd thought about and said to Tira over John. How she must have suffered through that mockery of a marriage, and how horrible if she'd loved John. She must have had her illusions shattered. She was the injured party. But Simon had taken John's side and punished her as if she was guilty for John's death. He'd deliberately put her out of his life, forbidding her to come close, even to touch him.

He closed his eyes in anguish. She would never let him near her again, no matter how he apologized. He'd said too much, done too much. She'd loved him, and he'd savaged her. And it had all been for nothing. She'd been innocent.

He finished his drink with dead eyes. Regrets seemed to pile up in the loneliness of the night. He glanced toward the Christmas tree his enthusiastic housekeeper had set up by the window, and dreaded the whole holiday season. He'd spend Christmas alone. Tira, at least, would have the despised Charles Percy for company.

He wondered why she didn't marry the damned man. They seemed to live in each others' pockets. He remembered that Charles had always been her champion, bolstering her up, protecting her. Charles had been her friend when Simon had turned his back on her, so how could he blame her for preferring the younger man?

He put his glass down and got to his feet. He felt every year of his age. He was almost forty and he had nothing to show for his own life. The child he might have had was gone, along with Melia, who'd never loved him. He'd lived on illusions of love for a long time, when the reality of love had ached for him and he'd turned his back.

If he'd let Tira love him...

He groaned aloud. He might as well put that hope to rest right now. She'd hate him forever and he had only himself to blame. Perhaps he deserved her hatred. God knew, he'd hurt her enough.

He went to bed, to lie awake all night with the memory of Tira's wounded eyes and drawn face to haunt him.

Five

Simon was not in a good mood the next morning when he went into work. Mrs. Mackey, his middle-aged secretary, stopped him at the door of his office with an urgent message to call the governor's office as soon as he came in. He knew what it was about and he groaned inwardly. He didn't want to be attorney general, but he knew for a fact that Wally was going to offer it to him. Wallace Bingley was a hard man to refuse, and he was a very popular governor as well as a friend. Both Simon and Tira had been actively involved in his gubernatorial campaign.

"All right, Mrs. Mack," he murmured, smiling as he used her nickname, "get him for me."

She grinned, because she knew, too, what was going on.

Minutes later, the call was put through to his office.

"Hi, Wally," Simon said. "What can I do for you?"

"You know the answer to that already," came the wry response. "Will you or won't you?"

"I'd like a week or so to think about it," Simon said seriously. "It's a part of my life I hadn't planned to take up again. I don't like living in a goldfish bowl and I hear it's open season on attorneys general in Texas."

Wallace chuckled. "You don't have as many political enemies as he does, and you're craftier, too. All right, think about it. Take the rest of the month. But two weeks is all you've got. After the holidays, his resignation takes effect, and I have to appoint someone."

"I promise to let you know by then," Simon assured him.

"Now, to better things. Are you coming to the Starks's Christmas party?"

"I'd have liked to, but my brothers are throwing a party down in Jacobsville and I more or less promised to show up."

"Speaking of the 'fearsome four,' how are they?"

"Desperate." Simon chuckled. "Corrigan phoned day before yesterday and announced that Dorie thinks she's pregnant. If she is, the boys are going to have to find a new victim to make biscuits for them."

"Why don't they hire a cook?"

"They can't keep one. You know why," Simon replied dryly.

"I guess I do. He hasn't changed."

"He never will," Simon agreed, referring to his brother Leopold, who was mischievous and sometimes outrageous in his treatment of housekeepers. Unlike the other two of the three remaining Hart bachelor brothers, Callaghan and Reynard, Leopold was a live wire.

"How's Tira?" Wallace asked unexpectedly. "I hear her showing was a huge success."

The mention of it was uncomfortable. It reminded him all too vividly of the mistakes he'd made with Tira. "I suppose she's fine," Simon said through his teeth.

"Er, well, sorry, I forgot. The publicity must have been hard on both of you. Not that anybody takes it seriously. It certainly won't hurt your political chances, if that's why you're hesitating to accept the position."

"It wasn't. I'll talk to you soon, Wally, and thanks for the offer."

"I hope you'll accept. I could use you."

"I'll let you know."

He said goodbye and hung up, glaring out the window as he recalled what he'd learned about Tira so unexpectedly. It hurt him to talk about her now. It would take a long time for her to forgive him, if she ever did.

If only there was some way that he could talk to her, persuade her to listen to him. He'd tried phoning from home early this very morning. As soon as she'd heard his voice, she'd hung up, and the answering machine had been turned on when he tried again. There was no point in leaving a message. She was determined to wipe him right out of her life, apparently. He felt so disheartened he didn't know what to try next.

And then he remembered Sherry Walker, a mutual friend of his and Tira's in the past who loved opera and had season tickets in the aisle right next to his, in the dress circle. He knew that Sherry had broken a leg skiing just recently and had said that she wasn't leaving the house until it healed completely. Perhaps, he told himself, there was a way to get Tira to talk to him after all.

* * *

The letdown after the showing made Tira miserable. She had nothing to do just now, with the holiday season in full swing, and she had no one to buy a present for except Mrs. Lester and Charles. She went from store to colorfully decorated store and watched mothers and fathers with their children and choked on her own pain. She wouldn't have children or the big family she'd always craved. She'd live and die alone.

As she stood at a toy store window, watching the electric train sets flashing around a display of papier mache mountains and small buildings, she wondered what it would be like to have children to buy those trains for.

A lone, salty tear ran down her cold-flushed cheek and even as she caught it on her knuckles, she felt a sudden pervasive warmth at her back.

Her heart jumped even before she looked up. She always knew when Simon was anywhere nearby. It was a sort of unwanted radar and just lately it was more painful than ever.

"Nice, aren't they?" he asked quietly. "When I was a boy, my father bought my brothers and me a set of 'O' scale Lionel trains. We used to sit and run them by the hour in the dark, with all the little buildings lighted, and imagine little people living there." He turned, resplendant in a charcoal gray cashmere overcoat over his navy blue suit. His white shirt was spotless, like the patterned navy-and-white tie he wore with it. He looked devastating. And he was still wearing the hated prosthesis.

"Isn't this a little out of your way?" she asked tautly.

"I like toy stores. Apparently so do you." He searched what he could see of her averted face. Her glorious hair was in a long braid today and she was wearing a green silk pantsuit several shades darker than her eyes under her long black leather coat.

"Toys are for children," she said coldly.

He frowned slightly. "Don't you like children?"

She clenched her teeth and stared at the train. "What would be the point?" she asked. "I won't have any. If you'll excuse me..."

He moved in front of her, blocking the way. "Doesn't Charles want a family?"

It was a pointed question, and probably taunting. Charles's brother was still in the hospital and no better, and from what Charles had been told, he might not get better. There was a lot of damage to Gene's heart. Charles would be taking care of Nessa, whom he loved, but Simon knew nothing about that.

"I've never asked Charles how he feels about children," she said carelessly.

"Shouldn't you? It's an issue that needs to be resolved before two people make a firm commitment to each other."

Was he deliberately trying to lacerate her feelings? She wouldn't put it past him now. "Simon, none of this is any of your business," she said in a choked tone. "Now will you please let me go?" she asked on a nervous laugh. "I have shopping to do."

His good hand reached out to lightly touch her shoulder, but she jerked back from him as if he had a communicable disease.

"Don't!" she said sharply. "Don't ever do that!"

He withdrew his hand, scowling down at her. She was white in the face and barely able to breathe from the look of her.

"Just...leave me alone, okay?" She choked, and

darted past him and into the thick of the holiday crowd
on the sidewalk. She couldn't bear to let her weakness
for him show. Every time he touched her, she felt vi-
brations all the way to her toes and she couldn't hide
it. Fortunately she was away before he noticed that it
wasn't revulsion that had torn her from his side. She
was spared a little of her pride.

Simon watched her go with welling sadness. It could
have been so different, he thought, if he'd been less
judgmental, if he'd ever bothered to ask her side of her
brief marriage. But he hadn't. He'd condemned her on
the spot, and kept pushing her away for years. How
could he expect to get back on any sort of friendly
footing with her easily? It was going to take a long
time, and from what he'd just seen, his was an uphill
climb all the way. He went back to his office so de-
jected that Mrs. Mack asked if he needed some aspirin.

Tira brushed off the chance meeting with Simon as
a coincidence and was cheered by an unexpected call
from an old friend, who offered her a ticket to *Tur-
andot,* her favorite opera, the next evening.

She accepted with pure pleasure. It would do her
good to get out of the house and do something she
enjoyed.

She put on a pretty black designer dress with dia-
manté straps and covered it with her flashy velvet wrap.
She didn't look half bad for an old girl, she told her
reflection in the mirror. But then, she had nobody to
dress up for, so what did it matter?

She hired a cab to take her downtown because finding a parking space for the visiting opera performance
would be a nightmare. She stepped out of the cab into
a crowd of other music lovers and some of her painful

loneliness drifted away in the excitement of the performance.

The seat she'd been given was in the dress circle. She remembered so many nights being here with Simon, but his reserved seat, thank God, was empty. If she'd thought there was a chance of his being here, she'd never have come. But she knew that Simon had taken Jill to see this performance already. It was unlikely that he'd want to sit through it again.

There was a drumroll. The theater went dark. The curtain started to rise. The orchestra began to play the overture. She relaxed with her small evening bag in her lap and smiled as she anticipated a joyful experience.

And then everything went suddenly wrong. There was a movement to her left and when she turned her head, there was Simon, dashing in dark evening clothes, sitting down right beside her.

He gave her a deliberately careless glance and a curt nod and then turned his attention back to the stage.

Tira's hands clenched on the evening bag. Simon's shoulder brushed against hers as he shifted in his seat and she felt the touch as if it were fire all the way down her body. It had never been so bad before. She'd walked with him, talked with him, shared seats at benefits and auctions and operas and plays with him, and even though his presence had been a bittersweet delight, it had never been so physically painful to her in the past. She wanted to turn and find his mouth with her lips, she wanted to press her body to his and feel his cheek against her own. The longing so was poignant that she shivered with it.

"Cold?" he whispered.

She clenched her jaw. "Not at all," she muttered, sliding further into her velvet wrap.

His good arm went, unobtrusively, over the back of her seat and rested there. She froze in place, barely daring to move, to breathe. It was just like the afternoon in front of the toy store. Did he know that it was torture for her to be close to him? Probably he did. He'd found a new way to get to her, to make her pay for all the terrible things he thought she'd done. She closed her eyes and groaned silently.

The opera, beautiful as it was, was forgotten. She was so miserable that she sat stiffly and heard none of it. All she could think about was how to escape.

She started to get up and Simon's big hand caught her shoulder a little too firmly.

"Stay where you are," he said gruffly.

She hesitated, but only for an instant. She was desperate to escape now. "I have to go to the necessary room, if you don't mind," she bit off near his ear.

"Oh."

He sighed heavily and moved his arm, turning to allow her to get past him. She apologized all the way down the row. Once she made it to the aisle, she felt safe. She didn't look back as she made her way gracefully and quickly to the back of the theater and into the lobby.

It was easy to dart out the door and hail a cab. This time of night, they were always a few of them cruising nearby. She climbed into the first one that stopped, gave him her address, and sat back with a relieved sigh. She'd done it. She was safe.

She went home more miserable than ever, changed into her nightgown and a silky white robe and let her hair down with a long sigh. She couldn't blame her friend, Sherry, for the fiasco. How could anyone have known that Simon would decide to see the opera a second time on this particular night? But it was a cruel blow of fate. Tira had looked forward to a performance that Simon's presence had ruined for her.

She made coffee, despite the late hour, and was sitting down in the living room to drink it when the doorbell rang.

It might be Charles, she decided. She hadn't heard from him today, and he could have stopped by to tell her about Gene. She went to the front door and opened it without thinking.

Simon was standing there with a furious expression on his face.

She tried to close the door, but one big well-shod foot was inside it before she could even move. He let himself in and closed the door behind him.

"Well, come in, then," she said curtly, her green eyes sparkling with bad temper as she pulled her robe closer around her.

He stared at her with open curiosity. He'd never seen her in night clothing before. The white robe emphasized her creamy skin, and the lace of her gown came barely high enough to cover the soft mounds of her breasts. With her red-gold hair loose in a glorious tangle around her shoulders, she was a picture to take a man's breath away.

"Why did you run?" he asked softly.

Her face colored gently. "I wasn't expecting you to be there," she said, and it came out almost as an accusation. "You've already seen the performance once."

"Yes, with Jill," he added deliberately, watching her face closely.

She averted her eyes. He looked so good in an eve-

ning jacket, she thought miserably. His dark, wavy hair
was faintly damp, as if the threatening clouds had let
some rain fall. His pale gray eyes were watchful, dis-
turbing. He'd never looked at her this way before, like
a predator with its prey. It made her nervous.

"Do you want some coffee?" she asked to break the
tense silence.

"If you don't put arsenic in it."

She glanced at him. "Don't tempt me."

She led him into the kitchen, got down a cup and
poured a cup of coffee for him. She didn't offer cream
and sugar, because she knew he took neither.

He turned a chair around and straddled it before he
picked up the cup and sipped the hot coffee, staring at
her disconcertingly over the rim.

With open curiosity, she glanced at the prosthesis
hand, which was resting on the back of the chair.

"Something wrong?" he asked.

She shrugged and picked up her own cup. "You
used to hate that." She indicated the artificial arm.

"I hate pity even more," he said flatly. "It looks
real enough to keep people from staring."

"Yes," she said. "It does look real."

He sipped coffee. "Even if it doesn't feel it," he
murmured dryly. He glanced up at her face and saw it
color from the faint insinuation in his deep voice.
"Amazing, that you can still blush, at your age," he
remarked.

It wouldn't have been if he knew how totally innocent she still was at her advanced age, but she wasn't
sharing her most closely guarded secret with the enemy. He thought she and Charles were lovers, and she
was content to let him. But that insinuation about why
he used the prosthesis was embarrassing and infuriat-

ing. She hated being jealous. She had to conceal it from him.

"I don't care how it feels, or to whom," she said stiffly. "In fact, I have no interest whatsoever in your personal life. Not anymore."

He drew in a long breath and let it out. "Yes, I know." He finished his coffee in two swallows. "I miss you," he said simply. "Nothing is the same."

Her heart jumped but she kept her eyes down so that he wouldn't see how much pleasure the statement gave her. "We were friends. I'm sure you have plenty of others. Including Jill."

His intake of breath was audible. "I didn't realize how much you and Jill disliked each other."

"What difference does it make?" She glanced at him with a mocking smile. "I'm not part of your life."

"You were," he returned solemnly. "I didn't realize how much a part of it you were, until it was too late."

"Some things are better left alone," she said evasively. "More coffee?"

He shook his head. "It keeps me awake. Wally called and offered me the attorney general's post," he said. "I've got two weeks to think about it."

"You were a good attorney general," she recalled. "You got a lot of excellent legislation through the general assembly."

He smiled faintly, studying his coffee cup. "I lived in a goldfish bowl. I didn't like it."

"You have to take the bad with the good."

He looked at her closely. "Tell me what happened the night they took you to the hospital."

She shrugged. "I got drunk and passed out."

"And the pistol?"

"The mouse." She nodded toward the refrigerator.

"He's under there, I can hear him. He can't be trapped and he's brazen. I got drunk and decided to take him out like John Wayne, with a six-shooter. I missed."

He chuckled softly. "I thought it was something like that. You're not suicidal."

"You're the only person who thinks so. Even Dr. Gaines didn't believe me. He wanted me to have therapy," she scoffed.

"The newspapers had a field day. I guess Jill helped feed the fire."

She glanced up, surprised. "You knew?"

"Not until she commented on it, when it was too late to do anything. For what it's worth," he added quietly, "I don't know many people who believed the accounts in her cousin's paper."

She leaned back in her chair and stared at him levelly. "That I did it for love of you?" she drawled with a poisonous smile. "You hurt my feelings when you accused me of killing my husband," she said flatly. "I was already overworked and depressed and I did something stupid. But I hope you don't believe that I sit around nights crying in my beer because of unrequited passion for you!"

Her tone hit him on the raw. He got slowly to his feet and his eyes narrowed as he stared down at her.

She felt at a distinct disadvantage. She'd only seen Simon lose his temper once. She'd never forgotten and she didn't want to repeat the experience.

"It's late," she said quickly. "I'd like to go to bed."

"Would you really?" His pale gaze slid over her body as he said it, his voice so sensuous that it made her bare toes curl up on the spotless linoleum floor.

She didn't trust that look. She started past him and found one of her hands suddenly trapped by his big one. He moved in, easing her hand up onto the silky fabric of his vest, inside it against the silky warmth of his body under the thin cotton shirt. She could feel the springy hair under it as well, and the hard beat of his heart as his breath whispered out at her temple, stirring her hair. She'd never been so close to him. It was as if her senses, numb for years, all came to life at once and exploded in a shattering rush of physical sensation. It frightened her and she pushed at his chest.

"Simon, let go!" she said huskily, all in a rush.

He didn't. He couldn't. The feel of her in his arms exceeded his wildest imaginings. She was soft and warm and she smelled of flowers. He drank in the scent and felt her begin to tremble. It went right to his head. His hand left hers and slid into her hair at her nape, clenching, so that she was helpless against him. He fought for control. He mustn't do this. It was too soon. Far too soon.

His breath came quickly. She could hear it, feel it. His cheek brushed against hers roughly, as if he wanted to feel the very texture of her skin there. He had a faint growth of beard and it rasped a little, but it was more sensual than uncomfortable.

Her heart raced as wildly as his. She wanted to draw back, to run, but that merciless hand wasn't unclenching. If anything, it had an even tighter grip on her long hair.

She wasn't protesting anymore. He felt her yield and his body clenched. His cheek drew slowly against hers. She felt his mouth at the corner of her own, felt his breath as his lips parted.

"Don't..." The little cry was all but inaudible.

"It's too late," he said roughly. "Years too late. God, Tira, turn your mouth against mine!"

She heard the soft, gruff command with a sense of total unreality. Her cold hands pressed against his shirtfront, but it was, as he said, already too late.

He moved his head just a fraction of an inch, and his hard, hot mouth moved completely onto hers, parting her lips as it explored, settled, demanded. There was a faint hesitation, almost of shock, as sensual electricity flashed between them. He felt her mouth tremble, tasted it, savored it, devoured it.

He groaned as his mouth began to part her lips insistently. Then his arm was around her, the one with the prosthesis holding her waist firmly while the good one lifted and traced patterns from her cheek down to her soft, pulsing throat. He could hear the tortured sound of his own breath echoed by her own.

She whimpered as she felt the full force of his mouth, felt the kiss she'd dreamed of for so many years suddenly becoming reality. He tasted of coffee. His lips were hard and demanding on her mouth, sensual, insistent. She didn't protest. She clung to him, savoring the most ecstatic few seconds of her life as if she never expected to feel anything so powerful again.

Her response puzzled him, because it wasn't that of an experienced woman. She permitted him to kiss her, clung to him closely, even seemed to enjoy his rough ardor; but she gave nothing back. It was almost as if she didn't know how...

He drew back slowly. His pale, fierce eyes looked down into hers with pure sensual arrogance and more than a little curiosity.

This was a Simon she'd never seen, never known, a sensual man with expert knowledge of women that was evident even in such a relatively chaste encounter. She was afraid of him because she had no defense against that kind of ardor, and fear made her push at his chest.

He put her away from him abruptly and his arms fell to his sides. She moved back, her eyes like saucers in a flushed, feverish face, until she was leaning against the counter.

Simon watched her hungrily, his eyes on the noticeable signs of her arousal in her body under the thin silk gown, in her swollen mouth and the faint redness on her cheek where his own had rubbed against it with his faint growth of beard. He'd never dreamed that he and Tira would kindle such fires together. In all their years of careless friendship, he'd never really approached her physically until tonight. He felt as if he were drowning in uncharted waters.

Tira went slowly to the back door and opened it, unnaturally calm. She still looked gloriously beautiful, even more so because she was emotionally aroused.

He took the hint, but he paused at the open door to stare down at her averted face. She was very flustered for a woman who had a lover. He found himself bristling with sudden and unexpected jealousy of the most important man in her life.

"Lucky Charles," he said gruffly. "Is that what he gets?"

Her eyes flashed at him. "You get out of here!" she managed to say through her tight throat. She pulled her robe tight against her throat. "Go. Just, please, go!"

He walked past her, hesitating on the doorstep, but she closed the door after him and locked it. She went back through the kitchen and down the hall to her bedroom before she dared let the tears flow. She was too shaken to try to delve into his motives for that hungry kiss. But she knew it had to be some new sort of revenge for his friend John. Well, it wouldn't work! He was never going to hurt her again, she vowed. She only wished she hadn't been stupid enough to let him touch her in the first place.

Simon stood outside by his car in the misting rain, letting the coolness push away the flaring heat of his body. He shuddered as he leaned his forehead against the cold roof of the car and thanked God he'd managed to get out of there before he did something even more stupid than he already had.

Tira had submitted. He could have had her. He was barely able to draw back at all. What a revelation that had been, that a woman he'd known for years should be able to arouse such instant, sweeping passion in him. Even Melia hadn't had such a profound effect on him, in the days when he'd thought he loved her.

He hadn't meant to touch her. But her body, her exquisite body, in that thin robe and gown had driven him right over the edge. He still had the taste of her soft, sweet lips on his mouth, he could still feel her pressed completely to him. It was killing him!

He clenched his hand and forced himself to breathe slowly until he began to relax. At least she hadn't seen him helpless like this. If she knew how vulnerable he was, she might feel like a little revenge. He couldn't blame her, but his pride wouldn't stand it. She might decide to seduce him and then keep him dangling. That would be the cruelest blow of all, when he knew she was Charles Percy's lover. He had sick visions of Tira telling him everything Simon had done to her and laughing about how easily she'd knocked him off balance. Charles was Tira's lover. Her lover. God, the thought of it made him sick!

He could see why Charles couldn't keep away from her. It made him bitter to realize that he could probably have cut Charles out years ago if he hadn't been so blind and prejudiced. Tira could have been his. But instead, she was Charles's, and she could only hate Simon now for the treatment he'd dealt out to her. He couldn't imagine her still loving him, even if he had taunted her with it to salvage what was left of his pride.

He got into his car finally and drove away in a roar of fury. Damn her for making him lose his head, he thought, refusing to remember that he'd started the whole damned thing. And damn him for letting her do it!

Six

After consuming far more whiskey than he should have the night before, Simon awoke with vivid memories of Tira in his arms and groaned heavily. He'd blown it, all over again. He didn't know how he was going to smooth things over this time. Jill called and invited herself to lunch with him, fishing for clues to his unusual bad humor. He mumbled something about going to the opera and having an argument with Tira, but offered no details at all. She asked him if he'd expected Tira to be there, and he brushed off further questions, pleading work.

Jill was livid at the thought that Tira was cutting in on her territory, just when things were going so well. She phoned the house and was told by Mrs. Lester that Tira had gone shopping. The rest was easy....

Tira, still smoldering from the betrayal of her weak body the night before, treated herself to lunch at a small sandwich shop downtown. Fate seemed to be against her, she thought with cold resignation, when Jill Sinclair walked into the shop and made a beeline for her just as she was working on dessert and a second cup of coffee.

"Well, how are you doing?" Jill asked with an innocent smile. "Just sandwiches? Poor you! Simon's taking me to Chez Paul for crepes and cherries jubilee."

"Then why are you here?" Tira asked, not disposed to be friendly toward her worst enemy.

Jill's perfect eyebrows arched. "Why, I was shopping next door for a new diamond tennis bracelet and I spotted you in here," she lied. "I thought a word to the wise, you know," she added, glancing around with the wariness of a veteran intelligence agent before she leaned down to whisper, "Simon was very vexed to have found you sitting next to him at the opera last night. You really should be more careful about engineering these little 'accidental' meetings and chasing after him, dear. He's in a vicious mood today!"

"Good!" Tira said with barely controlled rage. She glared at the other woman. "Would you like to have coffee with me, Jill?" She asked, and drew back the hand that was holding the cup of lukewarm coffee. "Let me introduce you to Miss Cup!"

Jill barely stepped back in time as the coffee cup flew through the air and hit the floor inches in front of her. Her eyes were wide open, and her mouth joined it. She hadn't expected her worst enemy to fight back.

"My, my, aren't I the clumsy one!" Tira said sweetly. "I dropped Miss Cup and spilled my coffee!"

Jill swallowed, hard. "I'll just be off," she said quickly.

"Oh, look," Tira added, lifting the plastic coffeepot the waitress had left on her table with a whimsical smile. "Mr. Coffeepot's coming after Miss Cup!"

Jill actually ran. If Tira hadn't been so miserable, she might have laughed at the sight. As it was, she apologized profusely to the waitress about the spilled coffee and left a tip big enough to excuse the extra work she'd made for the woman.

But it didn't really cheer her up. She went back home and started sculpting a new piece for the gallery. It wasn't necessary work, but it gave her something to do so that she wouldn't spend the day remembering Simon's hard kisses or thinking about how good Jill would look buried up to her armpits in stinging nettles.

The next day she was asked to serve on a committee to oversee Christmas festivities for a local children's shelter. It was a committee that Simon chaired, and she refused politely, only to have him call her right back and ask why.

She was furious. "Don't you know?" she demanded. "You had Jill rub my nose in it for—how did she put this?—chasing you to the opera!"

There was a long pause. "I asked Sherry to give you the ticket to the opera, since she couldn't use it," he confessed, to her surprise. "If anyone was chasing, it was me."

She felt her heart stop. "What?"

"You heard me," he said curtly. There was another pause. "Work with me on the committee. You'll enjoy it."

She would. But she was reluctant to get closer to

him than a telephone receiver. "I don't know that I would," she said finally. "You're not yourself lately."

"I know that." He was feeling his way. "Can't we start again?"

She hesitated. "As what?" she asked bluntly.

"Co-workers. Friends. Whatever you like."

That was capitulation, of a sort, at least. Perhaps he was through trying to make her pay for John's untimely death. Whatever his reason, her life was empty without him, wasn't it? Surely friendship was better than nothing at all? She refused to think about how his kisses had felt.

"Is Jill on the committee?" she asked suddenly, wary of plots.

"No!"

That was definite enough. "All right, then," she said heavily. "I'll do it."

"Good! I'll pick you up for the meeting tomorrow night."

"No, you won't," she returned shortly. "I'll drive myself. Where is it?"

He told her. There was nothing in his voice to betray whether or not he was irritated by her stubborn refusal to ride with him. He was even more irritated by Jill's interference. He'd made a bad mistake there, taking out Tira's worst enemy. He'd been depressed and Jill was good company, but it would have to stop. Tira wasn't going to take kindly to having Jill antagonize her out of sheer rivalry.

Tira went to the meeting, finding several old friends serving on the committee. They worked for three hours on preparations for a party, complete with an elderly local man who had agreed to play Santa Claus for the children. Tira was to help serve and bring two cakes, having volunteered because she had no plans for Christmas Eve other than to lay a trap for that mouse in the kitchen. Another woman, a widow, also volunteered to help, and two of the men, including Simon.

He stopped her by her car after the meeting. "The boys are having a Christmas party Saturday night in Jacobsville. They'd like you to come."

"I don't…"

He put a big forefinger across her soft mouth, startling her. The intimacy was unfamiliar and worrisome.

"Charles can do without you for one Saturday night, can't he?" he asked curtly.

"I haven't seen Charles lately. His brother, Gene, is in the hospital," she said, having forgotten whether or not she'd mentioned it to him. "Nessa isn't coping well at all, and Charles can't leave her alone."

"Nessa?"

"Gene's wife." She wanted to tell him about Nessa and Charles, but it wasn't her secret and letting him think she and Charles were close was the only shield she had at the moment. She couldn't let her guard down. She still didn't quite trust him. His new attitude toward her was puzzling and she didn't understand why he'd changed.

"I see."

"You don't, but it doesn't matter. I want to go home. I'm cold."

He searched her quiet face. "I could offer an alternative," he said in a soft, velvety tone.

She looked up at him with cool disdain. "I don't do casual affairs, Simon," she said bluntly. "Just in case the thought had crossed your mind lately."

He looked as if he'd been slapped. His jaw tautened.

"Don't you? Then if your affair with Charles Percy isn't casual, why hasn't he married you?"

"I don't want to marry again," she said in a husky voice, averting her eyes. "Not ever."

He hesitated. He knew why she felt that way, that she'd been betrayed in the worst way. Her father-in-law had told him everything, but he was uncertain about whether or not to tell her that he knew.

She glanced at him warily. "Does Jill know that you're still grieving for your wife?" she asked, taking the fight right into the enemy camp. "Or is she just an occasional midnight snack?"

His eyebrows arched. "That's a hell of a comparison."

"Isn't it?" She smiled sweetly. "I'm going home."

"Come to Jacobsville with me."

"And into the jaws of death or kitchen slavery?" she taunted. "I know all about the biscuit mania. I'm not about to be captured by your loopy brothers."

"They won't come near you," he promised. "Corrigan's hired a new cook. She's redheaded and she can bake anything."

"She won't last two weeks before Leopold has her running for the border," she assured him.

It pleased him that she knew his brothers so well, that she took an interest in his family. She and Corrigan had been friends and occasionally had dated in the past, but there had been no spark between them. In fact, Charles Percy had always been in the way of any other man and Tira. Why hadn't he noticed that before?

"You've been going around with Charles ever since you left John," he recalled absently.

"Charles is my friend," she said.

"Friend," he scoffed, his eyes insulting. "Is that what it's called these days?"

"You should know," she returned. "What does Jill call it?"

His eyes narrowed angrily. "At least she's honest about what she wants from me," he replied. "And it isn't my money."

She shrugged. "To each his own."

He searched her face quietly. "You kissed me back the other night."

Her cheeks went ruddy and she looked away, clutching her purse. "I have to go."

He was right behind her. He didn't touch her, but she could feel the warm threat of him all down her spine, oddly comforting in the chilly December air.

"Stop running!"

Her eyes closed for an instant before she reached for the door handle. "We seemed to be friends once," she said in a husky tone. "But we weren't, not really. You only tolerated me. I'm amazed that I went through all those years so blind that I never saw the contempt you felt when you looked at me."

"Tira..."

She turned, holding up a hand. "I'm not accusing you. I just want you to know that I'm not carrying a torch for you or breaking my heart because you go around with Jill." Her eyes were lackluster and he realized with a start that she'd lost a lot of weight in the past few months. She looked fragile, breakable.

"What are you saying?" he asked.

"That I don't need you to pity me, Simon," she said with visible pride. "I don't really want a closer association with you, whatever Jill says or you think. I'm rearranging my life. I've started over. I don't want to go back to the way we were.''

He felt those words like a knife. She meant them. It was in her whole expression.

"I see," he said quietly.

"No, you don't," she replied heavily. "You're sort of like a drug," she mused. "I was addicted to you and I've been cured, but even small doses are dangerous to my recovery."

His heart leaped. He caught her gaze and held it relentlessly. "What did you say?"

"You know what I mean," she returned. "I'm not going to let myself become addicted again. I have Charles and you have Jill. Let's go our separate ways and get on with our lives. I was serious about the pistol and the mouse, you know, it wasn't some face-saving excuse. I never meant to kill myself over you."

"Oh, hell, I knew that."

"Then why..."

"Yes?"

She turned her purse in her hands. "Why do you keep engineering situations where we'll be thrown together?" she asked. "It serves no purpose."

His hand came out of his pocket and lifted to touch, lightly, her upswept hair. She flinched and he dropped his hand with a long sigh.

"You can't forget, can you?" he asked slowly.

"I'm trying," she assured him. "But every time we're together, people speculate. The newspaper stories were pretty hard to live down, even for me. I don't really want to rekindle speculation."

"You never cared about gossip before."

"I was never publicly savaged before," she countered. "I've been made to look like some clinging, simpering nymph crying for a man who doesn't want her. My pride is in shreds!''

He was watching her narrowly. "How do you know that I don't want you, Tira?'' he asked deliberately.

She stared at him without speaking, floored by the question.

"I'll pick you up at six on Saturday and drive you to Jacobsville," he said. "Wear something elegant. It's formal.''

"I won't go,'' she said through her teeth.

"You'll go,'' he replied with chilling certainty.

He turned and walked to his own car with her glaring after him. Well, they'd just see about that! she told herself.

It was barely a week until Christmas. Tira had the party for the children to look forward to on Christmas Eve, to help her feel some Christmas spirit. She had an artificial tree that she set up in her living room every year. She'd have loved a real one, with its own dirt ball so that it could be set out in the yard after the holidays, but she was violently allergic to fir trees of any kind. The expensive artificial tree was very authentic-looking and once she decorated it, it could have fooled an expert at a distance.

She had a collection of faux gold-plated cherubs and elegant gold foil ribbons to use for decorations, along with gold and silver bead strands and fairy lights. For whimsy, there were a few mechanical ornaments scattered deep within the limbs, which could be activated by the touch of a finger. She had a red-and-white latch-hook rug that went around the base of the tree, and around that was a Lionel "O" scale train set—the one she'd seen in the window of the department store that day she'd come across Simon on the sidewalk. She'd gone back and bought the train, and now she enjoyed watching it run. It only lacked one or two little lighted buildings to go beside it. Those, she reasoned, she could add later.

She stood back and admired her handiwork. She was wearing a gold-and-white caftan that echoed the color scheme of the tree, especially with her hair loose. It was Saturday, but she wasn't going to the Hart party. In fact, when Simon rang the doorbell, he wasn't going to get into the house. She felt very smug about the ease with which she'd avoided him.

"Very nice," came a deep, amused voice from behind her.

She whirled and found Simon, in evening clothing, watching her from the doorway.

"How…how did you get in?" she gasped.

"Mrs. Lester kindly left the back door unlocked for me," he mused. "I told her that we were going out and that you'd probably forget. She's very obliging. A real romantic, Mrs. Lester."

"I'll fire her Monday the minute she gets back from her sister's!" she snarled.

"No, you won't. She's a treasure."

She swept back her hair. "I'm not going to Jacobsville!"

"You are," he said. "Either you get dressed, or I dress you."

"Ha!" She folded her arms across her chest and dared him to do his worst.

The prospect seemed to amuse him. He took her by the arm with his good hand and led her down the hall to her bedroom, opened the door, put her in and closed it behind them. He'd already been here, she could tell, because a white strapless evening gown was laid out on the bed, along with filmy underthings that matched it.

"You…you invaded my bedroom!" she raged.

"Yes, I did. It was very educational. You don't dress like a siren at all. Most of your wardrobe seems to consist of cotton underthings and jeans and tank tops." He glanced at her. "I like that caftan you're wearing, but it's not quite appropriate for tonight's festivities."

"I'm not putting on that dress."

He chuckled softly. "You are. Sooner or later."

She started toward the door and found herself swept up against him, held firmly by that damned prosthesis that seemed to work every bit as well as the arm it had replaced.

"I'm not going to hurt you," he promised softly. "But you're going."

"I will…what are you…doing?"

She'd forgotten the front zip that kept the caftan on her. He released it with a minimum of fuss and the whole thing dropped to the floor, leaving her in her bare feet and nude except for her serviceable white briefs.

She gaped at him. He looked at her body with the appreciation of an artist, noting the creamy soft rise of her breasts with their tight rosy nipples and the supple curve of her waist that flared to rounded hips and long, elegant legs.

"Don't you…look at me!" she gasped, trying to cover herself.

His eyes met hers quizzically. "Don't you want me to?" he asked softly.

The question surprised her. She only stared at him, watching his gaze fall again to her nudity and sweep

over it with pure delight. She shivered at the feel of
his gaze.

"It's all right," he said gently, surprised by the way
she was reacting. "I'm not even going to touch you. I
promise."

She drew in a shaky breath, held close by one arm
while his other hand traced along her flushed cheek and
down to the corner of her tremulous mouth.

What an unexpected creature she was, he thought
with some confusion. She was embarrassed, shy, even
a little ashamed to stand here this way. She blushed
like a girl. He knew that she couldn't be totally innocent, but her reaction was nothing like that of an experienced woman.

His fingers traced over her mouth and down the
curve of her pulsating throat to her collarbone. They
hesitated there and his gaze fell to her mouth.

The silence in the bedroom was like the silence in
the eye of a hurricane. If she breathed the wrong way,
it would break the spell, and he'd draw away. His fingers, even now, were hesitating at her collarbone and
his mouth hovered above hers as if he couldn't quite
decide what to do next.

She shivered, her own eyes lingering helplessly on
the long, wide curve of his mouth.

He moved, just slightly, so that her body was completely against his, and he let her feel the slow bur-
geoning of his arousal. It shocked her. He saw the flush
spread all over her high cheekbones.

"Tira," he said roughly, "tell me what you want."

"I don't…know," she whispered brokenly, searching his pale, glittering eyes. "I don't know!"

He felt her hips move, just a fraction, felt her body
shift so that she was faintly arched toward him. "Don't

you?'' he whispered back. ''Your body does. Shall I show you what it's asking me to do?''

She couldn't manage words, but he didn't seem to need them. With a faint smile, he lifted his hand and spread it against her rib cage, slowly, torturously sliding it up until it was resting just at the underside of her taut breast. She shivered and caught her breath, her eyes wide and hungry and still frightened.

''It won't hurt,'' he whispered, and his hand moved up and over her nipple, softly caressing.

She clutched his shoulders and hid her face against him in a torment of shattered sensations, moaning sharply at the intimate touch.

He hesitated. ''What's wrong?'' he asked gently. His face nuzzled against her cheek, forcing her head back so that he could see her shocked, helpless submission. He touched her again, easing his fingers together over the hard nipple as he tugged at it gently. The look on her face made his whole body go rigid.

Her head went back. Her eyes closed. She shivered, biting her lip to keep from weeping, the pleasure was so overwhelming.

If she was shaken, so was he. It was relatively chaste love play, but she was already reacting as if his body was intimately moving on hers. Her response was as unexpected as it was flattering.

''Come here,'' he said with rough urgency, tugging her to the bed. He pulled her down with him on the coverlet beside her gown and shifted so that she was beneath him. His rapid heartbeat was causing him to shake even before he found her mouth with his and began to caress her intimately.

''Simon,'' she sobbed. But she was pulling, not pushing. Her mouth opened for him, her body rose as he caressed it with his hand and then with his open mouth. He suckled her, groaning when she shivered and cried out from the pleasure. He was in so deep that he couldn't have pulled back to save his own life. He'd never known an exchange so heated, so erotic. He wanted to do things to and with her that he'd never dreamed of doing to a woman in his life.

His mouth eased back onto hers and gentled her as his hand moved under the elastic at her hips and descended slowly. Her legs parted for him. She gasped as he began to touch her, sobbed, wept, clutched him. She was ready for him, and he'd barely begun.

Even while his head spun with delight, he knew that it was wrong. It was all wrong. He'd been too long without a woman and this was too fiery, too consuming, for a first time with her. He was going in headfirst and she wouldn't enjoy it. But he couldn't stop himself.

"Tira," he groaned at her ear. "Sweetheart, not now. Not like this. For God's sake, help me...!"

His hand stilled, his mouth lay hot and hard against her throat while he lay against her, his big body faintly tremulous as he tried to overcome his urgent, aching need for her.

Seven

Tira barely heard him. Her body was shivering with new sensations, with exquisite glimpses of the pleasure he could offer her. She felt him go heavy in her arms and slowly, breath by breath, she began to realize where they were and what they were doing.

She caught her breath sharply, aware that her hands were still tangled in the thick, cool darkness of his wavy hair. She was almost completely nude and he'd touched her....

"Simon!" she exclaimed, aghast.

"Shhh." His mouth turned against her throat. His hand withdrew to her waist and his head lifted. He was breathing as raggedly as she was. The turbulence of his eyes surprised her, because his usual impeccable control was completely gone. He saw her expression and managed a smile. "Are you shocked that we could be like this, together?" he asked gently.

"Yes."

"So am I. But I don't want you like this, not in a fever so high that I can't think past relief," he said quietly. He moved away from her with obvious reluctance and took one last, sweeping glance at her yielded body before he sat up with his back to her and leaned forward to breathe.

She tugged the coverlet over her heated flesh and bit her swollen lips in an agony of shame and embarrassment. How in the world had *that* happened? If he hadn't stopped…!

He got to his feet, stretched hugely and then turned toward her. She lay with her glorious hair in a tangle around her white face, looking up at him almost fearfully.

"There's no need to look like that, Tira," he said softly, with eyes so tender that they confused her. He reached down and tugged the coverlet away, pulling her slowly to her feet. "The world won't end."

He reached for the strapless bra he'd taken from her bureau and using the prosthesis to anchor it, he looped it around her and held it in place.

"You'll have to fasten it," he said with a complete lack of self-consciousness. "I can't do operations that complex."

She obeyed him as if she were a puppet and he was pulling strings.

He held the half-slip and coaxed her to lean against him while she stepped into it. He pulled it up. He reached for the exquisite gown and deftly slid it over her head, watching while she tugged it into place. He turned her around and while she held up her hair, he zipped it into place.

He led her to the vanity and handed her a brush. She

sat down obediently and put her unruly hair back into some sort of order, belatedly using a faint pink lipstick and a little powder. He stood behind her the whole while, watching.

When she finished, he drew her up again and held her in front of him.

"How long have we known each other?" he asked solemnly.

"A long time. Years." She couldn't meet his probing gaze. She felt as if she had absolutely no will of her own. The sheer vulnerability was new and frightening. She took a deep breath. "We should go."

He tilted her remorseful eyes up to his. "Don't be ashamed of what we did together," he said quietly.

She winced. "You don't even like me...!"

He drew her close and rocked her against his tall body, his cheek pressed to her hair as he stroked the silken length of it. "Shhh." He kissed her hair and then her cheek, working his way up to her wet eyes. He kissed the tears away gently and then lifted his head and looked down into the drowned green depths. He couldn't remember ever feeling so tender with a woman. He remembered how her soft skin felt against his mouth and his breathing became labored. He stepped back a little, so that she wouldn't notice how easily she aroused him now.

She sniffed inelegantly and reached on the vanity for a tissue. "My nose will be as red as my eyes," she commented, trying to break the tension.

"As red as the highlights in your glorious hair," he murmured, touching it. He sighed. "I want you with me tonight," he said softly. "But if you really don't want to go, I won't force you."

She looked up, puzzled by his phrasing. "You said you would."

He frowned slightly. "I don't like making you cry," he said bluntly. "Until now, I didn't know that I could. It's uncomfortable."

"I've had a long week," she said evasively.

"We both have. Come with me. No strings. You'll have fun."

She hesitated, but only for a minute. "All right."

He reached down and curled her small hand into his big one. The contact was thrilling, exciting. She looked up into eyes that confused her.

"Don't think," he said. "Come along."

He pulled her along with him, out of the bedroom, out the door. It was new to have Simon act possessively about her, to be tender with her. It hurt terribly, in a way, because now she knew exactly what she'd missed in her life. Simon would be all she'd ever need, but she cared too much to settle for a casual affair. Regardless of what he thought of her marriage to John, and she had no reason to believe that he'd changed his mind about it, she did believe in marriage. She didn't want to be anyone's one-night stand; not even Simon's.

The long drive down to Jacobsville wasn't as harrowing as she'd expected it to be. Simon talked about politics and began asking pointed questions about an upcoming fund-raiser.

She wasn't comfortable with the new relationship between them, so when he asked if she might like to help with some projects for the governor if he took on the attorney general's job, she immediately suspected that he was using her helpless attraction to him to win her support.

She looked down at the small white beaded evening bag in her lap. "If I have time," she said, stalling.

He glanced at her as they passed through the gaily decorated downtown section of Jacobsville, dressed like a Christmas tree for the holidays with bright colored lights and tinsel.

"What else have you got to do lately?" he asked pointedly.

She stared at her bag. "I might do another exhibit."

He didn't ask again, but he looked thoughtful.

The Hart ranch was impressive, sprawling for miles, with the white fence that surrounded the house and immediate grounds draped with green garlands and artificial poinsettias.

"They haven't done that before," she commented as they went down the long paved driveway to the house.

"Oh, they've made a number of improvements since Dorie married Corrigan last Christmas and moved into their new house next door to this one," he explained.

"Reluctant improvements, if I know Callaghan."

He chuckled. "Cag doesn't go in much for frills."

"Is he still not eating pork?"

He gave her a wry glance. "Not yet."

It was a family joke that the eldest bachelor brother wouldn't touch any part of a pig since he'd seen the movie about the one that talked, a box office smash.

"I can't say that I blame him," she murmured. "I saw the movie three times myself."

He chuckled. It was a rare sound these days and she glanced at him with a longing that she quickly concealed when his eyes darted toward her.

He pulled up in front of the sprawling ranch house and got out, noting that Tira did the same without waiting for him to open her door. Her independent spirit irritated him at times, but he respected her for it.

When she started up the steps ahead of him, he caught her hand and kept it in his as they reached the porch, where Corrigan and Dorie greeted them with warm hugs and smiles. Tira smiled automatically, so aware of Simon's big hand in hers that she was almost floating.

"You're just in time," Corrigan said. "Leopold spiked the punch and didn't tell Tess, and she got the wrong side of Evan Tremayne's tongue. She's in the kitchen giving Leo hell and swearing that he'll never get another biscuit."

"He must be in tears by now," Simon mused.

"He's on his knees, in fact, groveling." Corrigan grinned. "It suits him."

They went inside, where they met Evan and his wife, Anna, who was obviously and joyfully pregnant with their first child, and the Ballenger brothers, Calhoun and Justin, with their wives Abby and Shelby, all headed toward the front door together. They were all founding families in the area, with tremendous wealth and power locally. Tira knew of them, but it was the first time she'd met them face-to-face. It didn't surprise her that the brothers had such contacts. They made friends despite their sometimes reclusive tendencies. All the same, the party looked as if it had only just started, and it puzzled her that these people were leaving so soon. They didn't seem angry, but with those bland expressions, it was sometimes hard to tell if they were.

Tira looked around for Cag and Rey and just spotted them going through the swinging door of the kitchen. In the open doorway she caught a glimpse of Leopold on his knees in a prayerful stance with a thin young redhead standing over him looking outraged.

Tira chuckled. Simon, having seen the same thing, laughed out loud.

"This is too good to miss. Come on." He nodded at other people he knew as they wove their way through the crowd and reached the kitchen.

Stealthily Simon pushed open the door. The sight that met their eyes was pitiful. Leopold was still on his knees, with Cag verbally flaying him while Rey looked on approvingly.

They glanced toward the door when Simon and Tira entered. Leopold actually blushed as he scrambled to his feet.

Tess grimaced as she spotted Simon, one of the only two brothers who actively intimidated her. "I don't care what they say, I'm quitting!" she told him despite her nervousness. "He—" she pointed at Leopold "—poured two bottles of vodka in my special tropical punch, and Evan Tremayne didn't realize it was spiked until he'd had his second glass and fell over a chair." She blushed. "He said terrible things to me! And he—" she pointed at Leopold again "—thought it was funny!"

"Evan Tremayne falling over a chair would make most people in Jacobsville giggle," Tira stated, "knowing how he hates alcohol."

"It gets worse," Tess continued, brushing back a short strand of red hair, her blue eyes flashing. "Evan thought the punch was so good that he gave a glass of it to Justin Ballenger."

"Oh, God," Simon groaned. "Two of the most fanatical teetotalers in the county."

"Justin got a guitar and started singing some Spanish song. Shelby dragged the guitar out of his hands just in time,'' Tess explained. She put her face in her hands. ''That was when Evan realized the punch was spiked and he said I should be strung up over the barn by my apron strings for doing such a nasty thing to your guests.''

''I'll speak to Evan.''

''Not now, you won't,'' Tira mentioned. ''We just met the Tremaynes going out the front door, along with both Ballenger brothers and their wives.''

''Oh, God!'' Leo groaned again.

''I'll phone him and apologize,'' Rey promised. ''I'll call them all and apologize. You can't leave!''

''Yes, I can. I quit.'' Tess had taken off her apron and thrown it at Leopold. ''You'd better learn how to bake biscuits, is all I can say. They—'' she pointed toward Cag and Rey ''—will probably kill you when I leave, and I'm glad! I hope they throw you out in the corral and let the crows eat you! That would get rid of two evils, because the crows will die of food poisoning for sure!''

She stormed through the door and Leopold groaned out loud. Cag's quiet eyes followed her and his face tautened curiously.

''Leo, how could you?'' Rey asked, aghast.

''It wasn't two bottles of vodka,'' he protested. ''It was one. And I meant to give it to Tess, just to irritate her, but I got sidetracked and Evan and Justin…well, you know.'' He brightened. ''At least Calhoun didn't get a taste of it!'' he added, as if that made things all right. Calhoun, once a playboy, was as bad as his brother about liquor since his marriage.

''He left, just the same. But you've got problems

closer to home. You'd better go after her," Simon pointed out.

"And fast!" Rey said through his teeth, black eyes flashing.

"Like a twister," Cag added with narrowed eyes. "If she leaves, you're going to get branded along with that stock I had shipped in today."

"I'm going, I'm going!" Leopold rushed out the back door after their housekeeper.

"Isn't she a little young for a housekeeper?" Simon asked his brothers. "She barely looks nineteen."

"She's twenty-two," Cag said. "Her dad was working for us when he dropped dead of a heart attack. There's no family and she can cook." His powerful shoulders lifted and fell. "It seemed an ideal solution. If we could just keep Leo away from her, things would be fine."

"Why does he have to torment the housekeepers all the time?" Rey asked miserably.

"He'll settle down one day," Cag murmured. He looked distracted, and he was glaring toward the back door. "He'd better not upset her again. In fact, I think I'll make sure he doesn't."

He nodded to the others and went after Leo and Tess.

"He's sweet on her," Rey said when the door closed behind him. "Not that he'll admit it. He thinks she's too young, and she's scared to death of him. She finds every sort of excuse to get out of the kitchen if he's the first one down in the mornings. It's sort of comical, in a way. I don't guess she knows that she could bring him to his knees with a smile."

"She's very young," Tira commented.

Rey glanced at her. "Yes, she is. Just what Cag needs, too, something to nurture. He's always bringing home stray kittens and puppies…just like her.'' He pointed to a small kitten curled up in a little bed in the corner of the kitchen. "She rescued the kitten from the highway. Cag bought the bed for it. They're a match made in heaven, but Leo's going to ruin everything. I think he's sweet on her, too, and trying to cut Cag out before she notices how much time he spends watching her.''

"This is not our problem,'' Simon assured his brother. "But I'd send Leo off to cooking school if I were you. No woman is ever going to be stupid enough to marry him and if he learns to make biscuits, you can do without housekeepers.''

"He made scrambled eggs one morning when Tess had to go to the eye doctor early to pick up her contacts,'' Rey said. "The dogs wouldn't even touch them!'' He glared at Tira and Simon and shrugged. "Come on. We've still got a few guests who haven't gone home. I'll introduce you to them.''

He led them into the other room and stopped suddenly, turning to look at them. "Wait a minute. Corrigan said you weren't speaking to each other after that newspaper stupidity.''

Simon still had Tira's slender hand tight in his. "A slight misunderstanding. We made up. Didn't we?'' he asked, looking down at Tira with an expression that made her face turn red.

Rey made a sound under his breath and quickly changed the subject.

Corrigan and Dorie joined them at the punch bowl, which had been refilled and dealcoholized. Dorie looked almost as pregnant as Anna Tremayne had, and she was radiant. Not even the thin scar on her delicate cheek could detract from her beauty.

"We'd almost given up hope," she murmured, laughing up at her adoring husband. "And then, wham!"

"We're over the moon," Corrigan said. The limp left over from his accident of years ago was much less noticeable now, he didn't even require a cane.

"I'm going to be an uncle," Simon murmured. "I might like that. I saw a terrific set of "O" scale electric trains in a San Antonio toy store a few days ago. Kids love trains."

"That's right, boys and girls alike," Tira murmured, not mentioning that she'd bought that train set for herself.

"Did you know that two of our local doctors, who are married to each other, have several layouts of them?" Corrigan murmured. "The doctors Coltrain. They invited kids from the local orphanage over for Christmas this year and have them set up and running. It's something of a local legend."

"I like trains," Simon said. "Remember that set Dad bought us?" he asked Corrigan.

"Yeah." The brothers shared a memory, not altogether a good one judging from their expression.

"This isn't spiked, anymore?" Tira asked, changing the subject as she stared at the punch bowl.

"I swear," Corrigan said, smiling affectionately at her. "Help yourself."

She did, filling one for Simon as well, and talk went to general subjects rather than personal ones.

The local live cowboy band played a slow, lazy tune and Simon pulled Tira onto the dance floor, wrapping her up tight in his arms.

The one with the prosthesis was a little uncomfortable and she moved imperceptibly.

"Too tight?" Simon asked softly, and let up on the pressure. "Sorry. I'm used to the damned thing, but I still can't quite judge how much pressure to use."

"It's all right. It didn't hurt."

He lifted his head and looked down into her eyes. "You're the only woman who's ever seen me without it," he mused. "In the hospital, when it was a stump—"

"You may have lost part of your arm, but you're alive," she interrupted. "If you hadn't been found for another hour, nothing would have saved you. As it was, you'd lost almost too much blood."

"You stayed with me," he recalled. "You made me fight. You made me live. I didn't want to."

She averted her eyes. "I know how much Melia meant to you, Simon. You don't have to remind me."

Secrets, he thought. There were so many secrets that he kept, that she didn't know about. Perhaps it kept the distance between them. It was time to shorten it.

"Melia had an abortion."

She didn't grasp what he was saying at first, and the lovely green eyes she lifted to his were curious. "What?"

"I made her pregnant and she ended it, and never told me," he said shortly. "She didn't want to ruin her figure. Of course, she wasn't positive that the baby was mine. It could have been by one of her other lovers."

She'd stopped dancing to stare up at him uncomprehendingly.

"She told me, the night of the accident," he contin-

ued. "That's why I lost control of the car in a curve,
in the rain, and I remember thinking in the split second
before it crashed that I didn't care to live with all my
illusions dead."

"Illusions?" she echoed.

"That my marriage was perfect," he said. "That my
beloved wife loved me equally, that she wanted my
children and a lifetime with only me." He laughed
coldly. "I married a cheap, selfish woman whose only
concern was living in luxury and notching her bedpost.
It excited her that she had men and I didn't know. She
had them in my bed." His voice choked with anger,
and he looked over her head. His arm had unconsciously tightened around Tira, and this time she didn't
protest. She was shocked by what he was telling her.
She'd thought, everyone had thought, that he'd buried
his heart in Melia's grave and had mourned her for
years.

"The child was what hurt the most," he said stiffly.
"I believed her when she said she thought she was
sterile. It was a lie. Everything she said was a lie, and
I was too besotted to realize it. She made a fool of
me."

"I'm so sorry for all the pain you've been through."
Her eyes filled with tears. "It must have been awful."

He looked down at her, his eyes narrow and probing.
"You were married to John when it happened. You
came to the hospital every day. You held my hand, my
good hand, and talked to me, forced me to get up, to
try. I always felt that you left John because of me, and
it made me feel guilty. I thought I'd broken up your
marriage."

She dropped her gaze to his strong neck. "No," she
said tersely. "You didn't break it up."

He curled her fingers into his and brought them to his chest, holding them there warmly. "Were you in love with him, at first?"

"I was attracted to him, very fond of him," she confessed softly. "And I wanted, badly, to make our marriage work." She shivered a little and he drew her closer. Her eyes closed. "I thought...I wasn't woman enough."

His indrawn breath was audible. He knew the truth about her marriage now, but he hesitated to bring up a painful subject again when things were going so well for them. His lips moved down to her eyes and kissed the eyelids with breathless tenderness.

"Don't cry," he said curtly. "You're more than woman enough. Come closer, and I'll prove it to you, right here."

"Simon..."

His arm slid down, unobtrusively, and drew her hips firmly against his. He shuddered as the touch of her body produced an immediate, violent effect.

She gasped, but he wouldn't let her step back.

"Do you feel how much I want you?" he whispered in her ear. "I've barely touched you and I'm capable."

"You're a man..."

"It doesn't, it never has, happened that fast with anyone else," he said through his teeth. "I want you so badly that it hurts like hell. Yes, Tira, you're woman enough for any man. I'm sorry that your husband didn't... No, that's a lie." He lifted his head and looked into her shocked eyes. "I'm glad he couldn't have you."

The words went right over her head because she was so shocked at what he was saying. She stared at him in evident confusion and embarrassment, her eyes darting around to see if anyone was watching. Nobody was.

"It doesn't show. There's no reason to be so tense." His arm moved back up to her waist and loosened a little.

She drew in steadying breaths, but she felt weak. Her head went to his chest and she made a plaintive little sound against it.

His fingers contracted around hers. "We opened Pandora's box together in your bedroom, on your bed," he whispered at her ear. "We want each other, Tira."

She swallowed. "I can't."

"Why not?"

She hesitated, but only for an instant. "I don't have affairs, Simon."

"Of course you do, darling," he drawled with barely concealed jealousy. "What else do you have with Charles Percy?"

Eight

Tira stopped dancing. She wasn't sure why she was upset, because Simon had made no bones about thinking she was sleeping with Charles. Apparently when he'd made light love to her earlier, he'd thought her responses were those of an experienced woman. She wondered what he'd think if he knew the truth, that she'd waited for him all these years, that she wanted no other man.

"Go ahead," he invited, a strange light in his eyes. "Deny it."

She let her gaze fall to his wide, firm mouth. "Think what you like," she invited. "You will anyway. And I'll remind you, Simon, that you have no right to question me about Charles."

"No right? After what you let me do to you?"

She flushed and her teeth clenched. "One weak moment..."

"Weak, the devil," he muttered quietly. "You were starving to death. Doesn't he make love to you anymore?"

"Simon, please don't," she pleaded. "Not tonight."

The hand holding hers contracted. "Were you thinking of him, then?"

"Heavens, no!" she burst out, aghast.

He searched her eyes for a long moment, until he saw her cheeks flush. His hand relaxed.

"I wasn't the only one who was starving," she murmured, a little embarrassed.

He coaxed her cheek onto his chest. "No, you weren't," he agreed. He closed his eyes as they moved to the music.

She was surprised that he could admit his own hunger. They were moving into a totally new relationship. She didn't know what to make of it, and she didn't quite trust him, either. But what she was feeling was so delicious that she couldn't fight it. She let her body go lax against him and breathed in the spicy scent of his cologne. Her hand moved gently against his shirt, feeling hair and hard, warm muscle under it. He stiffened and it delighted her that he could react so strongly to such an innocent caress.

"You'd better not," he whispered at her ear.

Her hand stilled. "Are you...hairy all over?" she whispered back.

He stiffened even more. "In places."

Her cheek moved against his chest and she sighed. "I'm sleepy," she murmured, closing her eyes as they moved lazily to the music.

"Want to go home?"

"We haven't been here very long."

"It doesn't matter. I've had a hard week, too." He

let her move away. "Come on. We'll make our excuses and leave."

They found Corrigan and asked him to tell the others Merry Christmas for them.

"They're still trying to talk Tess out of leaving," he murmured dryly. "I hope they can. The smell of baking biscuits makes Dorie sick right now," he said, glancing down at his wife lovingly. "So they'll have to go without if they can't change her mind."

"I wish them luck," Simon said. "We enjoyed the party. Next year, maybe I'll throw one and you can all come up to San Antonio for it."

"I'll hold you to that," Corrigan replied. He glanced from one of them to the other. "Have you two given up combat?"

"For the moment," Tira agreed with a wan smile.

"For good," Simon added.

"We'll see about that," Tira returned, her eyes flashing at him even through her fatigue.

They said their goodbyes and Simon drove them back to San Antonio. But instead of taking her home, he took her to his apartment.

She wondered why she didn't protest, which she certainly should have. She was too curious about why he'd come here.

"No questions?" he asked when they stepped out of the elevator on the penthouse floor.

"I suppose you'll tell me when you're ready," she replied, but with a faintly wary gaze.

"No need to worry," he said as he unlocked his door. "You won't get seduced unless you want to."

She blushed again and hated her own naivete. She followed him inside.

She'd never seen his apartment before. This was one

invitation she'd always hoped for and never got. Simon's private life was so private that even his brothers knew little of it.

The apartment was huge and furnished in browns and creams and oranges. He had large oil paintings, mostly of landscapes, on the walls, and the furniture had a vaguely Mediterranean look to it. It was heavy and old, and beautifully polished.

She ran her hand over the rosewood back of the green velvet-covered sofa that graced the living room. "This is beautiful," she commented.

"I hoped you might think so."

There was a long pause, during which she became more and more uncomfortable. She glanced at Simon and found him watching her with quiet, unblinking silvery eyes.

"You're making me nervous," she laughed unsteadily.

"Why?"

She shrugged in the folds of her velvet wrap. "I'm not sure."

He moved toward her with a walk that was as blatant as if he'd been whispering seductive comments to her. He took the cloak from her shoulders and the evening bag from her hands, tossing both onto the sofa. His jacket followed it. He took her hands and lifted them to his tie.

She hesitated. His fingers pressed her hands closer.

With breath that was coming hard and fast into her throat, she unfastened the silk tie and tossed it onto the sofa. He guided her fingers back to the top buttons of his shirt.

The silence in the apartment was tense, like the set of Simon's handsome, lean face. He stood quietly before her, letting her unfasten the shirt. But when she started to push it away, he shook his head.

"Looking at the prosthesis doesn't bother me," she said huskily.

"Humor me."

He drew her close and, pressing her fingers into the thick hair that covered his broad, muscular chest, he bent to her mouth.

His lips were tender and slow. He kissed her with something akin to reverence, brushing her nose with his as he made light contacts that provoked a new and sweeping longing for more.

Her fingers contracted in the hair on his chest and she went on tiptoe to coax his mouth harder against her own.

She felt his good hand on the zipper that held up her gown. She didn't protest as he slid it down and let the dress fall to the floor. She didn't protest, either, when he undid the catches to her longline bra with just the fingers of one hand. That, too, fell away and his gaze dropped hungrily to her pretty, taut breasts.

She stepped out of her shoes and he took her hand, pulling her along with him to his bedroom. It was decorated in the same earth tones as the living room. The bed was king-size, overlaid with a cream-and-brown striped quilted bedspread and a matching dust ruffle.

He reached behind him and closed the door, locking it as well.

She looked into his eyes with mingled hunger and apprehension. She knew exactly what he was going to do. She wanted to tell him how inexperienced she was, but she couldn't quite get the words out.

He led her to the bed and eased her down onto it. His hand went to his belt. He let his slacks fall to the floor and, clad only in black silk boxer shorts, he sat down on the bed and removed his shoes and socks.

"Your shirt," she whispered.

He eased down beside her, levering himself just above her at an angle. "I don't think I can do this without the prosthesis," he said quietly. "But I'd rather you didn't see it. Do you mind?"

She shook her head. He was devastating at close range. She loved the look of him, the feel of his hand on her face, her throat, then suddenly whispering over her taut breasts.

She arched under even that light pressure and her hands clenched as she looked up at him.

"Are you going to let me take you?" he asked in a soft, blunt tone.

She bit her lower lip worriedly. "Simon, I'm not sure—"

"Yes, you are," he interrupted. "You want me every bit as badly as I want you."

She still hesitated, but then she spoke. "Yes, I do." that was all she said—she couldn't tell him her secret yet.

He touched the hard tip of her breast and watched her shiver. "You beautiful creature," he said half under his breath. "I only hope I can do you justice."

While she was searching for the right words to make her confession, his head bent and his mouth suddenly opened right on her breast.

She caught his head, her nails biting into his scalp.

He lifted himself just enough to see her worried eyes. "I'm only going to suckle you," he said with soft surprise, wondering what sort of lover Charles Percy must have been to make her so afraid. "I won't hurt you."

He bent again, and this time she didn't protest. She couldn't. It was so sweet that it made her head spin to feel his hot, hard, moist mouth closing over the tight nipple. She moaned under her breath and writhed with pleasure. He nibbled her for a long time, moving slowly from one breast to the other while his hand traced erotic patterns on her belly and the insides of her thighs.

She barely noticed when he removed her briefs and then his own. His practiced caresses overwhelmed her. She was so enthralled by them that she ached to know him completely.

A long, feverish few minutes later, he moved between her long legs and his mouth pushed hard against her lips as his hips eased down against hers and he penetrated her.

The sensation was shocking, frightening. She drifted from a euphoric tension to harsh pain. Her nails bit into his broad shoulders and she called his name. But he was in over his head, all too quickly. He groaned harshly and pushed harder, crying out as he felt her envelope him.

"Oh...!" she sobbed, pushing against his chest.

He stilled for an instant, shuddering, and lifted tortured eyes to hers. "I'm hurting you?" he whispered shakenly. "Dear God...no, sweetheart!...don't move like that...!"

She shifted her hips in an effort to avoid the pain, and her sharp movements took him right over the edge.

His face tautened. He pushed, hard, his body totally out of control. "Oh, God, Tira, I'm so sorry...!" he said through his teeth, his eyes closed, his body suddenly urgent on hers.

He whispered it constantly until he completed his

possession of her, and seconds later, he arched and shuddered and cried out in a hoarse groan as completion left him exhausted and shivering on her damp body.

She felt him relax heavily onto her damp skin, so that she could barely breathe for the weight. She wept silently at the reality of intimacy. It wasn't glorious fireworks of ecstasy at all. It was just a painful way to give a man pleasure. She hated him. She hated herself more for giving in.

"Please," she choked. "Let me go."

There was a pause. He drew in a long breath. "Not on your life," he said huskily.

He lifted his head and stared into her eyes with an expression on his lean face that she couldn't begin to understand.

"Charles Percy," he said deliberately, "is definitely not your lover."

She swallowed and her face flamed. "I...I never said he was, not really," she stammered.

He supported himself on the prosthesis and looked down at what he could see of her damp, shivering body. He touched her delicately on her stomach and then trailed his hand down to her thighs. There was a smear of blood on them that seemed to capture his attention for a moment.

"Simon, it hurts," she whispered, embarrassed.

His eyes went back to hers. "I know," he replied gently. His hand moved gently between her long legs to where their bodies were still completely joined, and she caught his wrist, gasping.

"Shhh," he whispered. Ignoring her protests, he began to touch her.

Shocked at the sudden burst of unexpected pleasure,

her wide eyes went homing to his. Her mouth opened
as the breath came careening out of her. She caught his
shoulders again, digging her nails in. This was...it
was... Her eyes closed and she moaned harshly and
shivered.

"That's it," he whispered, easing his mouth down
onto hers as she shivered and shivered again. "This
isn't going to hurt. Open your mouth. I want you to
know me completely, in every way there is." His hips
moved slowly, and he felt her whole body jump as his
sensual caresses began to kindle a frightening sweet
tension in her. "I'm going to teach you to feel pleasure."

She gripped his shoulders and held on, her eyes
closed as his mouth worked its way even deeper into
her own. She moved her legs around his muscular
thighs to help him, to bring him into even closer contact, and gasped when she felt his invasion of her grow
even more powerful, more insistent. The pain was still
there, but it didn't matter anymore, because there was
such pleasure overlaying it. She wanted him!

She heard her own voice sobbing, pleading with him,
as the frenzy of pleasure grew to unbearable propor-
tions. She was beyond pride, beyond protest. He was
giving her pleasure of a sort she'd never dreamed existed. She belonged to him, was part of him, owned by
him.

His movements grew urgent, deep. He whispered
something into her open mouth but she couldn't hear
him anymore. She was focused on some dark, sweet
goal, every muscle straining toward it, her heartbeat
pulsing in time with it, her tense body lifting to meet
his as she pleaded for it.

His hips shifted all at once in a violent, hard rhythm

that brought the ecstasy rushing over her like a wave of white-hot sensation. She cried out endlessly as it swept her away, her body pressing to his in a convulsive arch as the pleasure went on and on and on and she couldn't get close enough…!

This time, she didn't feel the weight of him as he collapsed onto her exhausted body. She held him tightly, pulsing in the soft aftermath, her legs trembling as they curled around his. She could hear his ragged breathing as she heard her own.

A long time later, he lifted his head and looked down into her wide eyes. He smiled at the faint shock in them. "Yes," he whispered. "It was good, wasn't it?"

She made an embarrassed sound and hid her face against him.

He smiled against her hair. "I thought it would never stop," he whispered huskily, brushing damp strands of hair away from her lips, her eyes as he turned her toward him. "I've never been fulfilled so completely in all my life."

She searched his eyes, seeing such tenderness in them that she felt warm all over. She reached up and touched his damp face with pure wonder, from his thick eyebrows to his wide, firm mouth and his stubborn chin. She couldn't even speak.

"You must be the only twenty-eight-year-old virgin in Texas," he murmured, and he wasn't joking. His eyes were solemn. "Did you save it for me, all these years?"

She didn't want to admit that. He probably guessed that she had, but only a little pride remained in her arsenal.

She sighed quietly. "I never knew a man that I wanted enough," she confessed, averting a direct answer. She dropped her gaze to his broad, bare chest where the thick hair was damp with sweat. "I suppose you've lost count of all the women you've had in the past few years."

His finger traced her soft mouth. "I haven't had a woman since Melia died. I dated Jill, but we were never intimate."

Her surprise was all too evident as she met his rueful gaze. "What?"

His powerful shoulders rose and fell. "A one-armed man isn't a lover many women would choose. I've been sensitive about it, and perhaps a little standoffish when it came to invitations." He searched her eyes. "I've always been comfortable with you. I knew that if I fumbled, you wouldn't laugh at me."

"Never that," she agreed quietly. She looked at the way they were laying and flushed.

"Now you know," he murmured with a warm smile.

"Yes. Now I know."

"I'm sorry I had to hurt you." Regret was in his eyes as well as his tone. He traced her eyebrows. "It had been too long and I lost control. I couldn't pull away."

"I understood."

"You were tight," he said bluntly. "And very much a virgin. I apologize wholeheartedly for every nasty insinuation I've ever made about you."

She was uncomfortable. Was he apologizing for making love to her?

He tilted her face back up to his and kissed her tenderly. "I won't say I'm sorry," he whispered into her mouth. "You can't imagine how it felt, to know I was the first with you."

She frowned worriedly.

He lifted his head and saw her expression. "What's wrong?" he asked.

"You didn't use anything," she said.

"No. I assumed that you were on the pill," he replied. "That went along with the assumption that you were sleeping with Charles and you'd never gotten pregnant."

The very word made her flush even more. "Well, I'm not," she faltered.

An expression crossed his face that she couldn't understand. He looked down at her body pressed so closely, so intimately to his, and curiously, his big hand smoothed over her flat belly in a strangely protective caress.

"If I made you pregnant…"

He didn't have to finish the sentence. She always seemed to know what he was thinking. She reached up and put her cool fingers against his wide mouth.

"You know me," she whispered, anticipating the question he was afraid to ask.

He sighed and let the worry flow out of him. He bent to her mouth and traced it with his lips. "It would complicate things."

She only smiled. "Yes."

His mouth pressed down hard on hers all at once and his hips moved suggestively.

She cried out.

He stilled instantly, because it wasn't a cry of pleasure. "This is uncomfortable for you now," he said speculatively.

"It is," she confessed reluctantly. "I'm sorry."

"No, I'm sorry that I hurt you." He lifted his weight away and met her eyes. "It may be uncomfortable when I withdraw. I'll be as slow as I can."

The blunt remark made her cheeks go hot, but she watched him lift away from her with frank curiosity and a little awe.

"Oh, my," she whispered when he rolled over onto his back.

"Yes, isn't it shocking?" he whispered and pulled her gently against his side. "And now you know why it was so uncomfortable, don't you?" he teased softly.

She laid her cheek on his broad shoulder. "I have seen the occasional centerfold," she murmured, embarrassed. "Although I have to admit that they weren't in your class!"

He chuckled and took a deep, slow breath. "Your body will adjust to me."

That sounded as if he didn't mean tonight to be an isolated incident, and she frowned, because it worried her. She didn't want to be his mistress. Did he think that she'd agreed to some casual sexual relationship because she'd given in to his ardor?

His hand smoothed over her long, graceful fingers. "When you heal a little, I'll teach you how to give it back," he murmured sleepily. "That was the first thing I noticed when I kissed you," he added. "You didn't fight me, but you didn't respond, either."

She sighed. "I didn't know how," she said honestly. Her wide eyes stared across his chest to the big, dark bureau against the wall. Her nails scraped through the thick hair on his chest and she felt him move sinuously, as if he enjoyed it.

His hand pressed hers closer and he stretched, shivering a little in the aftermath. "I'd forgotten how good it could be," he murmured. He tugged on a damp strand of red-gold hair. "I'm not taking you home."

She stiffened. "But I..."

"But, nothing. You're mine. I'm not letting you go."

That sounded possessive. Perhaps it was a sexual thing that men felt afterward. She knew so little about intimacy and how men reacted to it.

As if he sensed her concern, he eased her over onto her side so that he could see her face. It disturbed him to see her expression.

"This was a mistake," he said at once when he saw her eyes. "Probably my biggest in a long line of them." His big hand pressed hard against her stomach. "But we're going to make it right. If you've got my baby in here, there's no way you're raising it alone. We'll get married as soon as I can get a license."

She was even more shocked by that statement than if he'd asked her to live in sin with him.

She took a breath and hesitated.

His eyes held hers firmly. "Do you want my baby?"

The way he said it made delicious chills run down her spine. There was all the tenderness in the world in the soft question, and tears stung her eyes.

"Oh, yes," she whispered.

He looked at her until her breathing changed, his eyes solemn and possessive as they trailed down to her submissive body and her soft, pretty breasts. He touched them delicately.

"Then we won't use anything," he murmured, lifting his eyes back to hers.

Her lips parted. There were so many questions spinning around in her mind that she couldn't grasp one to single out.

His fingers went up to her lips and traced them very slowly. "Why did you give yourself to me?" he asked.

She stared at him worriedly. "I thought you knew."

"I hope I do." He looked worried now. "I really didn't have any intention of seducing you, in case you wondered. I was going to kiss you. Maybe a little more than just that," he added with a rueful smile. "But you came in here with me like a lamb," he said, as if it awed him that she'd yielded so easily. "You never protested once, until I hurt you." He grimaced and brought her hand to his mouth, kissing the palm hungrily. "I never thought it would hurt you so much!" he said, as if the memory itself was painful. "You cried and started moving, and I lost my head completely. I couldn't even stop..."

"But, it's...it's normal for it to be a little uncomfortable the first time," she said quickly, putting her fingers against his hard mouth. "Simon, some girls are just a little unlucky. I suppose I was one of them. It's all right."

He met her eyes. His were still turbulent. "I wouldn't have hurt you for the world," he whispered huskily. "I wanted you to feel what I was feeling. I wanted you to feel as if the sun had exploded inside you." His fingers tangled softly in her hair. "It was...never like that," he added in quiet wonder as he searched her eyes. "I never knew it could be." He bent and touched his mouth to hers with breathless tenderness. "Dear God, I wanted to cherish you, and I couldn't keep my head long enough! It should have been tender between us, as tender as I feel inside when I touch you. But it had been years, and I was like an animal. I thought you were experienced...!"

She drew his face down to hers and kissed his eyelids closed. Her lips touched softly all over his face, his cheeks, his nose, his hard mouth. She kissed him as if he needed comforting.

"You wanted me," she whispered against his ear as she held him to her. "I wanted you, too. It didn't hurt the second time."

His arms slid under her and he shivered. "It won't ever hurt again. I swear it."

Her legs curled into his and she smiled dreamily. He might not love her, but he felt something much more than physical desire for her. That long, stumbling speech had convinced her of one thing, at least. She would marry him. There was enough to build on.

"Simon?" she whispered.

"Hmmm?"

"I'll marry you."

His mouth turned against her warm throat. "Of course you will," he whispered tenderly.

She closed her eyes and linked her arms around him, her fingers encountering the leather strap of the prosthesis. "Why don't you take it off?" she murmured sleepily.

He lifted his head and frowned. "Tira..."

She sat up, proudly nude, and drew him up with her so that she could push the shirt away. She watched his teeth clench as she undid the straps and eased the artificial appliance away, along with the sleeve that covered the rest of his missing arm.

She drew it softly to her breasts and held it there, watching the expression that bloomed on his lean, hard face at the gesture.

"Yes, you still have feeling in it, don't you?" she murmured with the first glint of humor she'd felt in a long time as she saw the desire kindle in his pale eyes.

"There, and other places," he said tautly. "And you're walking wounded. Don't torture me."

"Okay." She pushed him back down and curled up against him with absolute trust.

She looked like a fairy lying there next to him, as natural as rain or sun with his torn body. He looked at her with open curiosity.

"Doesn't it bother you, really?" he asked.

She nuzzled closer. "Simon, would it bother you if I was missing an arm?" she asked unexpectedly.

He thought about that for a minute. "No."

"Then that answers your question." She smiled. "I'm sleepy."

He laughed softly. "So am I."

He reached up and turned off the lamp, drowsily pulling the covers over them.

She stiffened and he held her closer.

"What is it?" he asked quickly.

"Simon, do you have a housekeeper?"

"Sure. She comes in on Tuesdays and Thursdays." His mouth brushed her forehead. "It's Saturday night," he reminded her. "And we're engaged."

"Okay."

His arm gathered her even closer. "We'll get the license first thing Monday morning and we'll be married Thursday. Who do you want to stand up with us?"

"I suppose it will have to be your brothers," she groaned.

He grinned. "Just thank your lucky stars you didn't refuse to marry me. Remember what happened to Dorie?"

She did. She closed her eyes. "I'm thankful." She drank in the spicy scent of him. "Simon, are you sure?"

"I'm sure." He drew her closer. "And so are you. Go to sleep."

Nine

They got up and showered and then made breakfast together. Tira was still shy with him, after what they'd done, and he seemed to find it enchanting. He watched her fry bacon and scramble eggs while he made coffee. She was wearing one of his shirts and he was wearing only a pair of slacks.

"We'll make an economical couple," he mused. "I like the way you look in my shirts. We'll have to try a few more on you."

"I like the way you look without your shirt," she murmured, casting soft glances at him.

He wasn't wearing the prosthesis and he frowned, as if he wasn't certain whether she was teasing.

She took up the eggs, slid them onto the plate with the bacon, turned the burner off and went to him.

"You're still Simon," she said simply. "It never mattered to me. It never will, except that I'm sorry it had to happen to you." She touched his chest with soft, tender hands. "I like looking at you," she told him honestly. "I wasn't teasing."

He looked at her in the morning light with eyes that puzzled her. He touched the glory of her long hair tenderly. "This is all wrong," he said quietly. "I should have taken you out, bought you roses and candy, called you at two in the morning just to talk. Then I should have bought a ring and asked you, very correctly, to marry me. I spoiled everything because I couldn't wait to get you into bed with me."

She was surprised that it worried him so much. She studied his hard face. "It's all right."

He drew in a harsh breath and bent to kiss her forehead tenderly. "I'm sorry, just the same."

She smiled and snuggled close to him. "I love you."

The words hit him right in the stomach. He drew in his breath as if he felt them. His hand tightened on her shoulder until it bruised. Inevitably he thought of all the wasted years when he'd kept her at a distance, treated her with contempt, ignored her.

"Hey." She laughed, wiggling.

He let go belatedly. His expression disturbed her. He didn't look like a happy prospective bridegroom. The eyes that met hers were oddly tortured.

He put her away from him with a forced smile that wouldn't have fooled a total stranger, much less Tira.

"Let's have breakfast."

"Of course."

They ate in silence, hardly speaking. He had a second cup of coffee and then excused himself while she put the breakfast things into the dishwasher.

She assumed that he was dressing and wanted her to do the same. She went back into the bedroom and quickly donned the clothing he'd removed the night before, having retrieved half of it from the living room. She didn't understand what was wrong with him, unless he really had lost his head and was now regretting everything including the marriage proposal. She knew from gossip that men often said things they didn't mean to make a woman go to bed with them. She must have been an easy mark, at that, so obviously in love with him that he knew she wouldn't resist him.

Last night it had seemed right and beautiful. This morning it seemed sordid and she felt cheap. Looking at herself in his mirror, she saw the new maturity in her face and eyes and mourned the hopeful young woman who'd come home with him.

He paused in the doorway, watching her. He was fully dressed, right down to the prosthesis.

"I'll take you home," he said quietly.

She turned, without looking at him. "That would be best."

He drove her there in a silence as profound as the one they'd shared over breakfast. When he pulled into her driveway, she held up a hand when he started to cut off the engine.

"You don't need to walk me to the door," she said formally. "I'll...see you."

She scrambled out of the car and slammed the door behind her, all but running for her front door.

The key wouldn't go in the first time, and she could hardly see the lock anyway for the tears.

She didn't realize that Simon had followed her until she felt his hand at her back, easing her inside the house.

"No, please..." she sobbed.

He pulled her into his arms and held her, rocked her, his lips in her hair.

"Sweetheart, don't," he whispered, his deep voice anguished. "It's all right! Don't cry!"

Which only made the tears fall faster. She cried until she was almost sick from crying, and when she finally lifted her head from his chest and saw his grim expression, it was all she could manage not to start again.

"I wish I could carry you," he murmured angrily, catching her by the hand to pull her toward the living room. "It used to give me a distinct advantage at times like these to have two good arms."

He sat down on the sofa and pulled her down into his lap, easing her into the elbow that was part prosthesis so that he could mop up her tears with his handkerchief.

"I don't even have to ask what you're thinking," he muttered irritably as he dried her eyes and nose. "I saw it all in my mirror. Good God, don't you think I'm sorry, too?"

"I know you are," she choked. "It's all right. You don't have to feel guilty. I could have said no."

He stilled. "Guilty about what?"

"Seducing me!"

"I didn't."

Her eyes opened wide and she gaped at him. "You did!"

"You never once said you didn't want to," he reminded her. "In fact, I distinctly remember asking if you did."

She flushed. "Well?"

"I don't feel guilty about *that*," he said curtly.

Her eyebrows lifted. "Then what are you sorry about?"

"That you had to come home in your evening gown feeling like a woman I bought for the night," he replied irritably. He touched her disheveled hair. "You didn't even have a brush or makeup with you."

She searched his face curiously. He was constantly surprising her these days.

He touched her unvarnished lips with a wry finger. "Now you're home," he said. "Go put on some jeans and a shirt and we'll go to Jacobsville and ride horses and have a picnic."

She lost her train of thought somewhere. "You want to take me riding?"

He let his gaze slide down her body and back up and his lips drew up into a sardonic smile. "On second thought, I guess that isn't a very good idea."

She realized belatedly what he was saying and flushed. "Simon!"

"Well, why dance around it? You're sore, aren't you?" he asked bluntly.

She averted her eyes. "Yes."

"We'll have the picnic, but we'll go in a truck when we get to the ranch."

She lifted her face back to his and searched his pale eyes. He looked older today, but more relaxed and approachable than she'd ever seen him. There were faint streaks of silver at his temples now, and silver threads mixed in with the jet black of his hair. She reached up and touched them.

"I'm almost forty," he said.

She bit her lower lip, thinking how many years had passed when they could have been like this, younger and looking forward to children, to a life together.

He drew her face to his chest and smoothed over her hair. She was so very fragile, so breakable now. He'd seen her as a flamboyant, independent, spirited woman who was stubborn and hot-tempered. And here she lay in his arms as if she were a child, trusting and gentle and so sweet that she made his heart ache.

He nuzzled his cheek against hers so that he could find her soft mouth, and he kissed it until a groan of anguish forced its way out of his throat. Oh, God, he thought, the years he'd wasted!

She heard the groan and drew back to look at him.

He was breathing roughly. His eyes, turbulent and fierce, lanced down into hers. He started to speak, just as the doorbell rang.

They both jumped at the unexpected loudness of it.

"That's probably Mrs. Lester," she said worriedly.

"On a Sunday? I thought she spent weekends with her sister?"

She did. Tira climbed out of his arms with warning bells going off in her head. She had a sick feeling that when she opened that door, her whole life was going to change.

And it did.

Charles Percy stood there with both hands in his pockets, looking ten years older and sick at heart.

"Charles!" she exclaimed, speechless.

His eyes ran over her clothing and his eyebrows arched. "Isn't it early for evening gowns?" He scowled. "Surely you aren't just getting home?"

"As a matter of fact, she is," Simon said from the doorway of the living room, and he looked more dangerous than Tira had ever seen him.

He approached Charles with unblinking irritation. "Isn't it early for you to be calling?" he asked pointedly.

"I have to talk to Tira," Charles said, obviously not understanding the situation at all. "It's urgent."

Simon leaned against the doorjamb and waved a hand in invitation.

Charles glared at him. "Alone," he emphasized. His scowl deepened. "And what are you doing here, anyway?" he added, having been so occupied with Gene and Nessa that he still thought Simon and Tira were feuding. "After what you and your vicious girlfriend said to her at the charity ball, I'm amazed she'll even speak to you."

Jill had gone right out of Tira's mind in the past twenty-four hours. Now she looked at Simon and remembered the other woman vividly, and a look of horror overtook her features.

Simon saw his life coming apart in those wide green eyes. Tira hadn't remembered Jill until now, thank God, but she was going to remember a lot more, thanks to Charles here. He glared at the man as if he'd have liked to punch him.

"Jill is part of the past," he said emphatically.

"Is she, really?" Charles asked haughtily. "That's funny. She's been hinting to all and sundry that you're about to pop the question."

Tira's face drained of color. She couldn't even look at Simon.

Simon called him a name that made her flush and caused Charles to stiffen his spine.

Charles opened the door wide. "I think this would be a good time to let Tira collect herself. Don't you?"

Simon didn't budge. "Tira, do you want me to leave?" he asked bluntly.

She still couldn't lift her eyes. "It might be best."

What a ghostly, thin little voice. The old Tira would

have laid about him with a baseball bat. But he'd weakened her, and now she thought he'd betrayed her. Jill had lied. If Tira loved him, why couldn't she see that? Why was she so ready to believe Charles?

Unless… He glared at the other man. Did she love Charles? Had she given in to a purely physical desire the night before and now she was ashamed and using Jill as an excuse?

"Please go, Simon," Tira said when he hesitated. She couldn't bear the thought that he'd seduced her on a whim and everything he'd said since was a lie. But how could Jill make up something as serious as an engagement? She put a hand to her head. She couldn't think straight!

Simon shot a cold glare at Tira and another one at Charles. He didn't say a single word as he stalked out the door to his car.

Tira served coffee in the living room, having changed into jeans and a sweater. She didn't dare think about what had happened or she'd go mad. Simon and Jill. Simon and Jill…

"What happened?" Charles asked curtly.

"One minute we were engaged and the next minute he was gone," she said, trying to make light of it.

"Engaged?"

She nodded, refusing to meet his eyes.

He put the evening gown and Simon's fury together and groaned. "Oh, no. Please tell me I didn't put my foot in it again?"

She shrugged. "If Jill says he's proposed to her, I don't know what to think. I guess I've been an idiot."

"I shouldn't have come. I shouldn't have opened my mouth." He put his face in his hands. "I'm so sorry."

"Why did you come?" she asked suddenly.

He drew his hands over his face, down to his chin. "Gene died this morning," he said gruffly. "I've just left Nessa with a nurse and made the arrangements at the funeral home. I came by to ask if you could stay with her tonight. She doesn't want to be alone, and for obvious reasons, I can't stay in my own house with her right now."

"You want me to stay with her in your house?" she asked.

He nodded. "Can you?"

"Charles, of course I can," she said, putting aside her own broken relationship for the moment. Charles's need was far greater. "I'll just pack a few things."

"I'll drive you over," he said. "You won't need your car until tomorrow. I'll bring you home then."

"Nessa can come with me," she said. "Mrs. Lester and I will take good care of her."

"That would be nice. But tonight, she doesn't need to be moved. She's sedated, and sleeping right now."

"Okay."

"Tira, do you want me to call Simon and explain, before we go?" he asked worriedly.

"No," she said. "It can wait."

Charles was the one in trouble right now. She refused to think about her own situation. She packed a bag, left a note for Mrs. Lester and locked the door behind them.

The next morning Mrs. Lester found only a hastily scribbled note saying that Tira had gone home with Charles—and not why. So when Simon called the next morning, she told him with obvious reluctance that apparently Tira had gone to spend the night at Charles's house and hadn't returned.

"I suppose it was his turn," he said with bridled fury, thanked her and hung up. He packed a bag without taking time to think things through and caught the next flight to Austin to see the governor about the job he'd been offered.

Gene's funeral was held on the Wednesday, and from the way Nessa clung to Charles, Tira knew that at least somebody's life was eventually going to work out. Having heard from Mrs. Lester that Simon had phoned and gone away furious having thought she spent the night with Charles, she had no hope at all for her own future.

She spent the next few days helping Nessa clear away Gene's things and get her life in some sort of order. Charles was more than willing to do what he could. By the time Christmas Eve rolled around, Tira was all by herself and so miserable that she felt like doing nothing but cry.

Nevertheless, she perked herself up, dressed in a neat red pantsuit and went to the orphans' Christmas party that she'd promised to attend.

She carried two cakes that she and Mrs. Lester had baked, along with all the paraphernalia that went with festive eats. Other people on the committee brought punch and cookies and candy, and there were plenty of gaily wrapped presents.

Tira hadn't expected to see Simon, and she didn't. But Jill, of all people, showed up with an armload of presents.

"Why, how lovely to see you, Tira," Jill exclaimed. She didn't get too close—she probably remembered the cup of coffee.

"Lovely to see you, too, Jill," Tira said with a noxious smile. "Do join the fun."

"Oh, I can't stay," she said quickly. "I'm filling in for Simon. Poor dear, he's got a raging headache and he couldn't make it."

"Simon doesn't have headaches," Tira said curtly, averting her eyes. "He gives them."

"I thought you knew he frequently gets them when he flies," Jill murmured condescendingly. "I've nursed him through several. Anyway, he just got back from Austin. He's accepted the appointment as attorney general, by the way." She sighed dramatically. "I'm to go with him to the governor's New Year's Ball! And I've got just the dress to wear, too!"

Tira wanted to go off and be sick. Her life had become a nightmare.

"Must run, dear," Jill said quickly. "I have to get home to Simon. Hope the party's a great success. See you!"

She was gone in the flash of an eye. Tira put on the best act she'd ever given for the orphans, handing out cake and presents with a smile that felt glued-on. The media showed up to film the event for the eleven o'clock news, as a human interest story, and Tira managed to keep her back to the cameras. She didn't want Simon to gloat if he saw how she really looked.

After the party, she wrapped herself in her leather coat, went home and threw up for half an hour. The nausea was new. She never got sick. There could only be one reason for it, and it wasn't anything she'd eaten. Two weeks into her only pregnancy with Tira, her mother had said, the nausea had been immediately apparent long before the doctors could tell she was pregnant.

Tira went to bed and cried herself to sleep. She did want the child, that was no lie, but she was so mad at Simon that she could have shot him. Poor little baby, to have such a lying pig for a father!

Just as she opened her eyes, there was a scratching sound and she looked up in time to see the unwelcome mouse, who'd been delightfully absent for two weeks, return like a bad penny. He scurried down the hall and she cursed under her breath. Well, now she had a mission again. She was going to get that mouse. Then she was going to get Simon!

She fixed herself a small milk shake for Christmas dinner and carried it to her studio. She wasn't even dressed festively. She was wearing jeans and a sweater and socks, with her hair brushed but not styled and no makeup on. She felt lousy and the milk shake was the only thing she could look at without throwing up.

Charles and Nessa had offered to let her spend Christmas with them, but she declined. The last thing she felt like was company.

She wandered through the studio looking at her latest creations. She sat down at her sculpting table and stared at the lump of clay under the wet cloth that she'd only started that morning. She wasn't really in the mood to work, least of all on Christmas Day, but she didn't feel like doing anything else, either.

Why, oh, why, had she gone to Simon's apartment? Why hadn't she insisted that he take her home? In fact, why hadn't she left him strictly alone after John died? She couldn't blame anyone for the mess her life was in. She'd brought it on herself by chasing after a man who didn't want her. Well, he did now—but only in one way. And after he married Jill…

She placed a protective hand over her stomach and sighed. She had the baby. She knew that she was pregnant. She'd have the tests, but they really weren't necessary. Already she could feel the life inside her instinctively, and she wondered if the baby would look like her or like Simon.

There was a loud tap at the back door. She frowned. Most people rang the doorbell. It wasn't likely to be Charles and Nessa, and it was completely out of the question that it could be Simon. Perhaps a lost traveler?

She got up, milk shake in hand, and went to the back door, slipping the chain before she opened it.

Simon stared down at her with quiet, unreadable eyes. He had dark circles under his eyes and new lines in his face. "It's Christmas," he said. "Do I get to come in?"

He was wearing a suit and tie. He looked elegant, hardly a match for her today.

She shrugged. "Suit yourself," she said tautly. She looked pointedly past him to see if he was alone.

His jaw tautened. "Did you expect me to bring someone?"

"I thought Jill might be with you," she said.

He actually flinched.

She let out a long breath. "Sorry. Your private life is none of my business," she said as she closed the door.

When she turned around, it was to find his hand clenched hard at his side.

"Speaking of private lives, where's Charles?" he asked icily.

She stared at him blankly. "With Nessa, of course."

He scowled. "What's he still doing with her?"

"Gene died and Nessa needs Charles now more than

ever.'' She frowned when he looked stunned. ''Charles
has been in love with Nessa for years. Gene tricked her
into marrying him, hoping to inherit her father's real
estate company. It went broke and he made Nessa his
scapegoat. She wouldn't leave him because she knew
he had a bad heart, and Charles almost went mad. Now
that Gene's gone, they'll marry as soon as they can.''

He looked puzzled. ''You went home with him...''

''I went to his house to stay with Nessa, the night
after Gene had died,'' she said flatly. ''Charles said that
it wouldn't look right for her to be there alone, and she
wouldn't stay at her own house.''

He averted his eyes. He couldn't look at her. Once
again, it seemed, he'd gotten the whole thing upside
down and made a mess of it.

''Why are you here?'' she asked with some of her
old hauteur. ''In case you were wondering, I'm not
going to shoot myself,'' she added sarcastically. ''I'm
through pining for you.''

He shoved his hand into his pocket and glanced toward her, noticing her sock-clad feet and the milk
shake in her hand. ''What's that?'' he asked suddenly.

''Lunch,'' she returned curtly.

His face changed. His eyes lifted to hers and he
didn't miss her paleness or the way she quickly avoided
meeting his searching gaze.

''No turkey and dressing?''

She shifted. ''No appetite,'' she returned.

He lifted an eyebrow and his eyes began to twinkle
as they dropped eloquently to her stomach. ''Really?''

She threw the milk shake at him. He ducked, but it
hit the kitchen cabinet in its plastic container and she
groaned at the mess she was going to have to clean up
later. Right now, though, it didn't matter.

"I hate you!" she raged. "You seduced me and then you ran like the yellow dog you are! You let Jill nurse you through headaches and spend Christmas Eve with you, and I hope you do marry her, you deserve each other, you...you...!"

She was sobbing by now, totally out of control, with tears streaming down her red face.

He drew her close to him and rocked her warmly, his hand smoothing her wild hair while she cried. "There, there," he whispered at her ear. "The first few months are hard, but it will get better. I'll buy you dill pickles and feed you ice cream and make dry toast and tea for you when you wake up in the morning feeling queasy."

She stilled against him. "W...what?"

"My baby, you're almost certainly pregnant," he whispered huskily, holding her closer. "From the look of things, very, very pregnant, and I feel like dancing on the lawn!"

Ten

She looked up at him with confusion, torn between breaking his neck and kissing him.

"Wh...what makes you think I'm pregnant?" she asked haughtily.

He smiled lazily. "The milk shake."

She shifted. "It's barely been two weeks."

"Two long, lonely weeks," he said heavily. He touched her hair, her face, as if he'd ached for her as badly as she had for him. "I can't seem to stop putting my foot in my mouth."

She lowered her eyes to his tie. It was a nice tie, she thought absently, touching its silky red surface. "You had company."

He tilted her face up to his eyes. "Jill likes to hurt you, doesn't she?" he asked quietly. "Why are you so willing to believe everything she says? I've never had any inclination to marry her, in the past or now. And as for her nursing me through a headache, you, of all people, should know I don't get them, ever."

"She said…!"

"I came home from Austin miserable and alone and I got drunk for the first time since the wreck," he said flatly. "She got in past the doorman at the hotel and announced that she'd come to nurse me. I had her shown to the front door."

Her eyebrows arched. That wasn't what Jill had said.

His eyes searched over her wan face. "And you don't believe me, do you?" he asked with resignation. "I can't blame you. I've done nothing but make mistakes with you, from the very beginning. I've lived my whole life keeping to myself, keeping people at bay. I loved Melia, in my way, but even she was never allowed as close as you got. Especially," he added huskily, "in bed."

"I don't understand."

His fingers traced her full lower lip. "I never completely lost control with her," he said softly. "The first time with you, I went right over the edge. I hurt you because I couldn't hold anything back." He smiled gently. "You didn't realize, did you?"

"I don't know much about…that."

"So I discovered." His jaw tautened as he looked at her. "Married but untouched."

Something niggled at the back of her mind, something he'd said about John. She couldn't remember it.

He bent and brushed his mouth gently over her forehead. "We have to get married," he whispered. "I want to bring our baby into the world under my name."

"Simon…"

He drew her close and his lips slid gently over her half-open mouth. She could feel his heartbeat go wild the minute he touched her. His big body actually trembled.

She looked up at him with quiet curiosity, seeing the raging desire he wasn't bothering to conceal blazing in his eyes, and her whole body stilled.

"That's right," he murmured. "Take a good look. I've managed to hide it from you for years, but there's no need now."

"You wanted me, before?" she asked.

"I wanted you the first time I saw you," he said huskily. His lean hand moved from her neck down to the hard peak of her breast visible under the sweater, and he brushed over it with his fingers, watching her shiver. "You were the most gloriously beautiful creature I'd ever seen. But I was married and I imagined that it was nothing more than the sort of lust a man occasionally feels for a totally inappropriate sort of woman."

"You thought I was cheap."

"No. I thought you were experienced," he said, and there was regret in his eyes. "I threw you at John to save myself, without having the first idea what I was about to subject you to. I'm sorry, if it matters. I never used to think of myself as the sort of man to run from trouble, but I spent years running from you."

She lowered her gaze to his tie again. Her heart was racing. He'd never spoken to her this way in the past. She felt his hand in her hair, tangling in it as if he loved its very feel, and her eyes closed at the tenderness in the caress.

"I don't want to be vulnerable," he said through his teeth. "Not like this."

She let out a long sigh. She understood what he meant. "Neither did I, all those years ago," she said heavily. "Charles was kind to me. He knew how I felt about you, and he provided me with the same sort of camouflage I gave him for Nessa's sake. Everyone thought we were lovers."

"I suppose you know I thought you were experienced when I took you to bed?"

She nodded.

"Even when you cried out, the first time, I thought it was pleasure, not pain. I'll never forget how I felt when I realized how wrong I'd been about you." His hand tightened on her soft body unconsciously. "I know how bad it was. Are you...all right?"

"Yes."

He drew her forehead against him and held it there while he fought for the right words to heal some of the damage he'd done. His eyes closed as he bent over her. It was like coming home. He'd never known a feeling like it.

She sighed and slid her arms under his and around him, giving him her weight.

He actually shivered.

She lifted her head and looked up, curious. His face was tight, his eyes brilliant with feeling. She didn't need a crystal ball to understand why. His very vulnerability knocked down all the barriers. She knew how proud he was, how he hated having her see him this way. But it was part of loving, a part he had yet to learn.

She took his hand in hers. "Come on," she said softly. "I can fix what's wrong with you."

"How do you know what's wrong with me?" he taunted.

She tugged at his hand. "Don't be silly."

She pulled him along with her out of the kitchen to

her bedroom and closed the door behind her. She was a little apprehensive. Despite the pleasure he'd given her, the memory of the pain was still very vivid.

He took a slow breath. "I'll always have to be careful with you," he said, as if he read the thoughts in her eyes. "I'm overendowed and you're pretty innocent, in spite of what we did together."

She blinked. "You...are?"

He scowled. "You said you'd seen centerfolds."

She colored wildly. "Not...of men...like that!"

"Well, well." He chuckled softly and moved closer to her. "I feel like a walking anatomy lab."

"Do you, really?" She drew his hand under her sweater and up to soft, warm skin, and shivered when he touched her. Her heart was in the eyes she lifted to his. "It won't hurt...?"

He drew her close and kissed her worried eyes shut. "No," he whispered tenderly. "I promise it won't!"

She let him undress her, still hesitant and shy with him, but obviously willing.

When she was down to her briefs, she began undressing him, to his amusement.

"This is new," he mused. "I've had to do it myself for a number of years."

She looked up, hesitating. "All that time," she said. "Didn't you want anyone?"

"I wanted you," he replied solemnly. "Sometimes, I wanted you desperately."

"You never even hinted...!"

"You know why," he said, as if it shamed him to remember. "I should have been shot."

She lowered her eyes to the bare, broad chest she'd uncovered. "That would have been a waste," she said with a husky note in her voice. Her fingers spread over the thick hair that covered him, and he groaned softly. She put her mouth against his breastbone. "I've missed you," she whispered, and her voice broke.

"I've missed you!"

He bent to her mouth and kissed her slowly, tenderly, while between them, they got the rest of the obstacles out of the way.

When she reached for the strap of the prosthesis, his fingers stayed her.

"We'll have to find out sometime if you can do without it," she said gently. Her eyes searched his. "You can always put it back on, if you have to."

He sighed heavily. "All right."

He let her take it off, the uncertainty plain in his dark face. It made him vulnerable somehow, and he felt vulnerable enough with his hunger for her blatantly clear.

She stretched out on the pale pink sheets and watched him come down to her with wide, curious eyes.

Amazingly he was able to balance, if a little heavily at first. But she helped him, her body stabilizing his as they kissed and touched in the most tender exchange of caresses they'd ever shared for long, achingly sweet minutes until the urgency began to break through.

It was tender even as he eased down against her and she felt him probing at her most secret place. She tensed, expecting pain, but it was easy now, if a little uncomfortable just at first.

He turned her face to his and made her watch his eyes as they moved together slowly. He pressed soft, quiet kisses against her mouth as the lazy tempo of his hips brought them into stark intimacy.

She gasped and pushed upward as the pleasure shot through her, but he shook his head, calming her.

"Wh...why?" she gasped.

"Because I want it to be intense," he whispered unsteadily, nuzzling her face with his as he fought for enough breath to speak. His teeth clenched as he felt the first deep bites of pleasure rippling through him. "I want it to take a long time. I want to...touch you...as deeply inside...as it's humanly possible!"

She felt him in every pore, every cell. Her fingers clenched behind his strong neck because he was even more potent now than he'd been their first time together. Her teeth worried her lower lip as she looked up at him, torn between pleasure and apprehension.

"Don't be afraid," he whispered brokenly. "Don't be afraid of me."

"It wasn't like this...before," she sobbed. Her eyes closed on a wave of pleasure so sharp that it stiffened her from head to toe. "Dear...God...Simon!"

"Baby," he choked at her ear. His body moved tenderly, even in its great urgency, from side to side, intensifying the pleasure, bringing her to the brink of some unbelievably deep chasm. She was going to fall...to fall...

She barely heard her own voice shattering into a thousand pieces as she reached up to him in an arc, sobbing, wanting more of him, more, ever more!

"Oh, God, don't...I'll hurt you!" he bit off as she pulled him down sharply to her.

"Never," she breathed. "Never! Oh, Simon...!"

She sobbed as the convulsions took her. It had never been this sweeping. Her eyes opened in the middle of the spasms and met his, and she saw in them the same helpless loss of control, the ecstasy that made a tight, agonized caricature of his face. It faded into a black oblivion as the pleasure became unbearable and she lost consciousness for a space of seconds.

"Tira? *Tira!*"

His hand was trembling as it touched her face, her neck where the pulse hammered.

"Oh, God, honey, open your eyes and look at me! Are you all right?"

She felt her eyelids part slowly. His face was above hers, worried, tormented, his eyes glittering with fear.

She smiled lazily. "Hello," she whispered, so exhausted that she could barely manage words. She moved and felt him deep in her body and moaned with pleasure.

"Good God, I thought I'd killed you!" he breathed, relaxing on her. He was heavy, and she loved his weight. She held him close, nuzzling her face into his cool, damp throat. "You fainted!"

"I couldn't help it," she murmured. "Oh, it was so good. So good, so good!"

He rolled over onto his back, carrying her with him. He shivered, too, as the movements kindled little skirls of pleasure.

She curled her legs into his and closed her eyes. "I love you," she whispered sleepily.

He drew in a shaky breath. "I noticed."

She kissed his neck lazily and sighed. "Simon, I think I really am pregnant."

"So do I."

She moved against him sinuously. "Are you sorry?"

"I'm overjoyed."

That sounded genuine, and reassuring.

"I'm sleepy."

He stretched under her. He'd used more muscles than he realized he had. "So am I."

It was the last thing she heard for a long time. When she woke again, she was under the sheet with her hair spread over the pillow. Simon was wearing everything but his jacket, and he was sitting on the edge of the bed just looking at her.

She opened her eyes and stared up at him. She'd never seen that expression on his face before. It wasn't one she could understand.

"Is something wrong?" she asked.

His hand went to her flat stomach over the sheet. "You don't think we hurt the baby?"

She smiled sleepily. "No. We didn't hurt the baby."

He wasn't quite convinced. "The way we loved this time..."

"Oh, that sounds nice," she murmured, smiling up at him with quiet, dreamy eyes.

His hand moved to hers and entangled with it. "What? That we loved?"

She nodded.

He drew their clasped hands to his broad thigh and studied them. "I've been thinking."

"What about?"

"It shouldn't be a quick ceremony in a justice of the peace's office," he said. He shrugged. "It should be in a church, with you in white satin."

"White? But..."

He lifted his eyes. They glittered at her. "White."

She swallowed. "Okay."

He relaxed a little. "I don't want people talking about you, as if we'd done something to be ashamed of—even though we have."

Her eyes opened wide. "What?"

"I used to go to church. I haven't forgotten how things are supposed to be done. We jumped the gun, twice, and I'm not very proud of it. But considering the circumstances, and this," he added gently, touching her belly with a curious little smile, "I think we're not quite beyond redemption."

"Of course we're not," she said softly. "God is a lot more understanding than most people are."

"And it isn't as if we aren't going to get married and give our baby a settled home and parents who love him," he continued. "So with all that in mind, I've put the wheels in motion."

"Wheels?"

He cleared his throat. "I phoned my brothers."

She sat straight up in bed with eyes like an owl's. "*Them?* You didn't! Simon, you couldn't!"

"There, there," he soothed her, "it won't be so bad. They're old hands at weddings. Look what a wonderful one they arranged for Corrigan. You went. So did I. It was great."

"They arranged Corrigan's wedding without any encouragement from Dorie at all! They kidnapped her and wrapped her in ribbons and carried her home to Corrigan for Christmas, for heaven's sake! I know all about those hooligans, and I can arrange my own wedding!" she burst out.

Just as she said that, the back door—the one they'd forgotten to lock—opened and they heard footsteps along with voices in the corridor.

The bedroom door flew open, and there they were, all of them except Corrigan. They stopped dead at the sight that met their eyes.

Cag glared at Simon. "You cad!" he snarled. "No

wonder you needed us to arrange a wedding! How could you do that to a nice girl like her?"

"Disgraceful," Leopold added, with a rakish grin. "Doesn't she look pretty like that?"

"Don't leer at your future sister-in-law," Rey muttered, hitting him with his Stetson. He put half a hand over his eyes. "Simon, we'd better do this quick."

"All we need is a dress size," Leopold said.

"I am not giving you my dress size, you hooligans!" Tira raged, embarrassed.

"Better get it one size larger, she's pregnant," Simon offered.

"Oh, thank you very much!" Tira exclaimed, horrified.

"You're welcome." He grinned, unrepentant.

"Pregnant?" three voices echoed.

The insults were even worse now, and Leopold began flogging Simon with that huge white Stetson.

"Oh, Lord!" Tira groaned, hiding her head in the hands propped on her upbent knees.

"It's a size ten," Rey called from the closet, where he'd been inspecting Tira's dresses. "We'd better make it a twelve. Lots of lace, too. We can get the same minister that married Corrigan and Dorie. And it had better be no later than three weeks," he added with a black glare at Simon. "Considering her condition!"

"It isn't a condition," Simon informed him curtly, "it's a baby!"

"And we thought they weren't speaking." Leopold grinned.

"We don't know yet that it's a baby," Tira said with a glare.

"She was having a milk shake for Christmas dinner," Simon told them.

"We saw it. Goes well with the cabinets, I thought," Rey commented.

"Don't worry, the mouse will eat it," Tira muttered.

"Mouse?" Cag asked.

"He can't be trapped or run out or baited," she sighed. "I've had three exterminators in. They've all given up. The mouse is still here."

"I'll bring Herman over," Cag said.

The others looked at him wide-eyed. "No!" they chorused.

"About the service," Simon diverted them, "we need to invite the governor and his staff—Wally said he'd give her away," he added, glancing at Tira.

"The governor is going to give me away? Our governor? The governor of our state?" Tira asked, aghast.

"Well, we've only got one." He grimaced. "Forgot to tell you, didn't I? I've accepted the attorney general slot. I hope you won't mind living in Austin."

"Austin."

She looked confused. Simon glanced at his brothers and waved his hand toward them. "Get busy, we haven't got a lot of time," he said. "And don't forget the media. It never hurts any political party to have coverage of a sentimental event."

"There he goes again, being a politician," Cag muttered.

"Well, he is, isn't he?" Rey chuckled. "Okay, boys, let's go. We've got a busy day ahead of us tomorrow. See you."

Cag hesitated as they went out the door. "This wasn't done properly," he told his brother. "Shame on you."

Simon actually blushed. "One day," he told the other man, "you'll understand."

"Don't count on it."

Cag closed the door, leaving two quiet people behind.

"He's never been in love," Simon murmured, staring at his feet. "He doesn't have a clue what it's like to want someone so bad that it makes you sick."

She stared at him curiously. "Is that how it was for you, today?"

"Today, and the first time," he said, turning his face to her. He searched her eyes quietly. "But in case you've been wondering, I'm not marrying you for sex."

"Oh."

He glowered. "Or for the baby. I want him very much, but I would have married you if there wasn't going to be one."

She was really confused now. Did this mean what it sounded like? No, it had to have something to do with politics. It certainly wouldn't hurt his standing in the political arena to have a pregnant, pretty, capable wife beside him, especially when there was controversy.

That was when the reality of their situation hit her. She was going to marry a public official, not a local attorney. He was going to be appointed attorney general to fill the present unexpired term, but he'd have to run for the office the following year. They'd live in a goldfish bowl.

She stared at him with horror in every single line of her face as the implications hit her like a ton of bricks. She sat straight up in bed, with the sheet clutched to her breasts, and stared at Simon horrified. He didn't know about John. Despite the enlightened times, some revelations could be extremely damaging, and not only to her and, consequently, Simon. There was John's fa-

ther, a successful businessman. How in the world
would it affect him to have the whole state know that
John had been gay?

The fear was a living, breathing thing. Simon had
no idea about all this. He hadn't spoken of John or
what he thought now that he knew Tira wasn't a murderess, but the truth could hurt him badly. It might hurt
the governor as well; the whole political party, in fact.

She bit her lip almost through and lowered her eyes
to the bed. "Simon, I can't marry you," she whispered
in a ghostly tone.

"You what?"

"You heard me. I can't marry you. I'm sorry."

He moved closer, and tilted her face up to his quiet
eyes. "Why not?"

"Because..." She hesitated. She didn't want to ever
have to tell him the truth about his best friend. "Because I don't want to live in a goldfish bowl," she lied.

He knew her now. He knew her right down to her
soul. He sighed and smiled at her warmly. "You mean,
you don't want to marry me because you're afraid the
truth about John will come to light and hurt me when
I run for office next year."

Eleven

She was so astonished that she couldn't even speak. "You...know?" she whispered.

He nodded. "I've known since that night at the gallery, when I spoke to your ex-father-in-law," he replied quietly. "He told me everything." His face hardened. "That was when I knew what I'd done to you, and to myself. That was when I hit rock bottom."

"But you never said a word..." Things came flying back into her mind. "Yes, you did," she contradicted herself. "You said that you were glad John couldn't have me...you knew then!"

He nodded. "It must have been sheer hell for you."

"I was fond of him," she said. "I would have tried to be a good wife. But I married him because I couldn't have you and it didn't really matter anymore." Her eyes were sad as they met his. "You loved Melia."

"I thought I did," he replied. "I loved an illusion,

a woman who only existed in my imagination. The reality was horrible.'' He reached out and touched her belly lightly, and she knew he was remembering.

Her fingers covered his. "You don't even have to ask how I feel about the baby, do you?''

He chuckled. "I never would have. You love kids.'' He grimaced. "I hated missing the Christmas Eve party. I watched you on television. I even knew why you kept your back to the camera. It was eloquent.''

"Jill has been a pain,'' she muttered.

"Not only for you,'' he agreed. He sighed softly. "Tira, I hope you know that there hasn't been anyone else.''

"It would have been hard to miss today,'' she said, and flushed a little.

He drew her across him and into the crook of his arm, studying her pretty face. "It doesn't bother you at all that I'm crippled, does it?''

"Crippled?'' she asked, as if the thought had never occurred to her.

That surprise was genuine. He leaned closer. "Sweetheart, I'm missing half my left arm,'' he said pointedly.

"Are you, really?'' She drew his head down to hers and kissed him warmly on his hard mouth. "You didn't need the prosthesis, either, did you?''

He chuckled against her lips. "Apparently not.'' His eyes shone warmly into hers. "How can you still love me after all I've put you through?'' he asked solemnly.

She let the sheet fall away from her high, pretty breasts and laid back against his arm to let him look. "Because you make love so nicely?''

He shook his head. "No, that's not it.'' He touched

her breasts, enjoying their immediate reaction. "Habit, perhaps. God knows, I don't deserve you."

She searched his face quietly. "I never knew you were vulnerable at all," she said, "that you could be tender, that you could laugh without being cynical. I never knew you at all."

"I didn't know you, either." He bent and kissed her softly. "What a lot of secrets we kept from each other."

She snuggled close. "What about John?" she asked worriedly. "If it comes out, it can hurt you and the party, it could even hurt John's father."

"You worry entirely too much," he said. "So what if it does? It's ancient history. I expect to be an exemplary attorney general—again—and what sort of pond scum would attack a beautiful pregnant woman?"

"I won't always be pregnant."

He lifted his head and gave her a wicked look. "No?"

She hit his chest. "I don't want to be the mother of a football team!"

"You'd love it," he returned, smiling at the radiance of her face. He chuckled. "I can see you already, letting them tackle you in mud puddles."

"They can tackle you. I'll carry the ball."

He glanced ruefully at the arm that was supporting her. "You might have to."

She touched his shoulder gently. "Does it really worry you so much?"

"It used to," he said honestly. "Until the first time you let me make love to you." He drew in a long breath. "You can't imagine how afraid I was to let you see the prosthesis. Then I was afraid to take it off, because I thought I might not be able to function as a man without using it for balance.''

"We'd have found a way," she said simply. "People do.''

He frowned slightly. "You make everything so easy.''

She lifted her fingers and smoothed away the frown. "Not everything. You don't feel trapped?''

He caught her hand and pulled the soft palm to his lips, kissing it with breathless tenderness. "I feel as if I've got the world in my arms," he returned huskily.

She smiled. "So do I.''

He looked as if he wanted to say something more, but he brought her close and wrapped her up against him instead.

The arrangements were complicated. Instead of a wedding, they seemed to be planning a political coup as well. The governor sent his private secretary and the brothers ended up in a furious fight with her over control of the event. It almost came to blows before Simon stepped in and reminded them that they couldn't plan the wedding without assistance. They informed him haughtily that they'd done it before. He threw up his hand and left them to it.

Tira had coffee with him in her living room in the midst of wedding invitations that she was hand signing. There must have been five hundred.

"I'm being buried," she said pointedly, gesturing toward the overflowing coffee table. "And that mouse is getting to me," she added. "I found *him* under one of the envelopes earlier!"

"Cag will take care of him while we're on our honeymoon. We can stay here until we find a house in Austin in a neighborhood you like.''

"One you like, too,'' she said.

"If you like it, so will I.''

It bothered her that he was letting her make all these decisions. She knew she was being cosseted, but she wasn't sure why.

"The brothers haven't been by today.''

"They're in a meeting with Miss Chase, slugging it out,'' he replied. "When I left, she was reaching for a vase.''

"Oh, dear.''

"She's a tough little bird. She's not going to let them turn our wedding into a circus.''

"They have fairly good taste,'' she admitted.

"They called Nashville to see how many country music stars they could hire to appear at the reception.''

"Oh, good Lord!'' she burst out.

"That isn't what Miss Chase said. She really needs to watch her language,'' he murmured. "Rey was turning red in the face when I ran for my life.''

"You don't run.''

"Only on occasion. Rey has the worst temper of the lot.''

"I'd put five dollars on Miss Chase,'' she giggled.

He watched her lift the cup to her lips. "Should you be drinking coffee?''

"It's decaf, darling,'' she teased.

The endearment caught him off guard. His breath caught in his throat.

The reaction surprised her, because he usually seemed so unassailable. She wasn't quite sure of herself even now. "If you don't like it, I won't...'' she began.

"Oh, I like it," he said huskily. "I'm not used to endearments, that's all."

"Yes, I know. You don't use them often."

"Only when I make love to you," he returned.

She lowered her eyes. He hadn't done that since the day they got engaged, when the brothers had burst into their lives again. She'd wondered why, but she was too shy to ask him.

"Hey," he said softly, coaxing her eyes up. "It isn't lack of interest. It's a lack of privacy."

She smiled wanly. "I wondered." She shrugged. "You haven't been around much."

"I've been trying to put together an office staff before I'm sworn in the first of January," he reminded her. "It's been a rush job."

"Of course. I know how much pressure you're under. If you'd like, we could postpone the wedding," she offered.

"Do you really want to be married in a maternity dress?" he teased.

Her reply was unexpected. She started crying.

He got up and pulled her up, wrapping her close. "It's nerves," he whispered. "They'll pass."

She didn't stop. The tears were worse.

"Tira?"

"I started," she sobbed.

"What?"

She looked up at him. Her eyes were swimming and red. "I'm not pregnant." She sounded as if the world had ended.

He pulled out a handkerchief and dried the tears. "I'm sorry," he whispered, and looked it. "I really am."

She took the handkerchief and made a better job of

her face, pressing her cheek against his chest. "I didn't know how to tell you. But now you know. So if you don't want to go through with it..."

He stiffened. His head lifted and he looked at her as if he thought she was possessed. "Why wouldn't I want to go through with it?" he burst out.

"Well, I'm not pregnant, Simon," she repeated.

He let out the breath he was holding. "I told you I wasn't marrying you because of the baby. But you weren't completely convinced, were you?"

She looked sheepish. "I had my doubts."

He searched her wet eyes slowly. He held her cheek in his big, warm hand and traced her mouth with his thumb. "I'm sorry that you aren't pregnant. I want a baby very much with you. But I'm marrying you because I love you. I thought you knew."

Her heart jumped into her throat. "You never said."

"Some words come harder than others for me," he replied. He drew in a long breath. "I thought, I hoped, you'd know by the way we were in bed together. I couldn't have been so out of control the first time or so tender the next if I hadn't loved you to distraction."

"I don't know much about intimacy."

"You'll learn a lot more pretty soon," he murmured dryly. He frowned quizzically. "You were going to marry me, thinking I only wanted you for the baby?"

"I love you," she said simply. "I thought, when the baby came, you might learn to love me." Her face dissolved again into tears. "And then...then I knew there wasn't going to be a baby."

He kissed her tenderly, sipping the tears from her wet eyes, smiling. "There will be," he whispered. "One day, I promise you, there will be. Right now, I only want to marry you and live with you and love you. The rest will fall into place all by itself.''

She looked into his eyes and felt the glory of it all the way to her soul. "I love you," she sobbed. "More than my life."

"That," he whispered as he bent to her mouth, "is exactly the way I feel about you!"

The wedding, despite the warring camps of its organizers, came off perfectly. It was a media event, at the ranch in Jacobsville, with all the leading families of the town in attendance and Tira glorious in a trailing white gown as she walked down the red carpet to the rose arbor where Simon and all his brothers and the minister waited. Dorie Hart was her matron of honor and the other Hart boys were best men.

The service was brief but eloquent, and when Simon placed the ring on her finger and then lifted her veil and kissed her, it was with such tenderness that she couldn't even manage to speak afterward. They went back down the aisle in a shower of rice and rose petals, laughing all the way.

The reception didn't have singers from Nashville. Instead the whole Jacobsville Symphony Orchestra turned out to play, and the food was flown in from San Antonio. It was a gala event and there were plenty of people present to enjoy it.

Tira hid a yawn and smiled apologetically at her new husband. "Sorry! I'm so tired and sleepy I can hardly stand up. I don't know what's wrong with me!"

"A nice Jamaican honeymoon is going to cure you of wanting sleep at all," he promised in a slow, deep drawl. "You are the most beautiful bride who ever walked down an aisle, and I'm the luckiest man alive."

She reached a hand up to his cheek and smiled lovingly at him. "I'm the luckiest woman."

He kissed her palm. "I wish we were ten years younger, Tira," he said with genuine regret. "I've wasted all that time."

"It wasn't wasted. It only made what we have so much better," she assured him.

"I hope we have fifty years," he said, and meant it.

They flew out late that night for their Caribbean destination. Cag, who hadn't forgotten the mouse, asked for the key to Tira's house and assured her that the mouse would be a memory when they returned. She had a prick of conscience, because in a way the mouse had brought her and Simon together. But it was for the best, she told herself. They couldn't go on living with a mouse! Although she did wonder what plan Cag had in mind that hadn't already been tried.

The Jamaican hotel where they stayed was right on the beach at Montego Bay, but they spent little time on the sand. Simon was ardent and inexhaustible, having kept his distance until the wedding.

He lay beside her, barely breathing after a marathon of passion that had left them both drenched in sweat and too tired to move.

"You need to take more vitamins," he teased, watching her yawn yet again. "You aren't keeping up with me."

She chuckled and rolled against him with a loving sigh. "It's the wedding and all the preparations," she whispered. "I'm just worn-out. Not that worn-out, though," she added, kissing his bare shoulder softly. "I love you, Simon."

He pulled her close. "I love you, Mrs. Hart. Very, very much."

She trailed her fingers across his broad, hair-roughened chest and wanted to say something else, but she fell asleep in the middle of it.

A short, blissful week later, they arrived back at her house with colorful T-shirts and wonderful memories.

"I could use some coffee," Simon said. "Want me to make it?"

"I'll do it, if you'll take the cases into the bedroom," she replied, heading for the kitchen.

She opened the cupboard to get out the coffee and came face-to-face with the biggest snake she'd ever seen in her life.

Simon heard a noise in the kitchen, put down the suitcases and went to see what had happened.

His heart jumped into his throat when he immediately connected the open cupboard, the huge snake and his new wife lying unconscious on the floor.

He bent, lifting her against his chest. "Tira, sweetheart, are you all right?" he asked softly, smoothing back her hair. "Can you hear me?"

She moved. Her eyelids fluttered and she opened her eyes, saw Simon, and immediately remembered why she was on the floor.

"Simon, there's a...a...*sssssssnake!*"

"Herman."

She stared at him. "There's a snake in the cupboard," she repeated.

"Herman," he repeated. "It's Cag's albino python."

"It's in *our* cupboard," she stated.

"Yes, I know. He brought it over to catch the mouse. Herman's a great mouser," he added. "Hell of a barrier to Cag's social life, but a really good mousetrap. We won't have a mouse now. Looks healthy, doesn't he?'' he added, nodding toward the cupboard.

While they were staring at the huge snake, the back door suddenly opened and Cag came in with a gunnysack. He saw Tira and Simon on the floor and groaned.

"Oh, God, I'm too late!" he said heartily. "I'm sorry, Tira, I let the time slip away from me. I forgot all about Herman until I remembered the date, and you'd already left the airport when I tried to catch you." He sighed worriedly. "I haven't killed you, have I?"

"Not at all," Tira assured him with grim humor. "I've been tired a lot lately, too. I guess I'm getting fragile in my old age."

Simon helped her to her feet, but he was watching her with a curious intensity. She made coffee while Cag got his scaly friend into a bag and assured her that she'd have no more mouse problems. Tira offered him coffee, but he declined, saying that he had to get Herman home before the big python got irritable. He was shedding, which was always a bad time to handle him.

"Any time would be a bad time for me," Tira told her husband when their guest had gone.

"You fainted," he said.

"Yes, I know. I was frightened."

"You've been overly tired and sleeping a lot, and I notice that you don't eat breakfast anymore." He caught her hand and pulled her down onto his lap. "You were sure you weren't pregnant. I'm sure you are. I want you to see a doctor."

"But I started," she tried to explain.

"I want you to see a doctor."

She nuzzled her face into his throat. "Okay," she said, and kissed him. "But I'm not getting my hopes up. It's probably just some female dysfunction."

The telephone rang in Simon's office, where he was winding up his partnership before getting ready to move into the state government office that had been provided for him.

"Hello," he murmured, only half listening.

"Mr. Hart, your wife's here," his secretary murmured with unusual dryness.

"Okay, Mrs. Mack, send her in."

"I, uh, think you should come out, sir."

"What? Oh. Very well."

His mind was still on the brief he'd been preparing, so when he opened the door he wasn't expecting the surprise he got.

Tira was standing there in a very becoming maternity dress, and had an ear-to-ear smile on her face.

"It's weeks too early, but I don't care. The doctor says I'm pregnant and I'm wearing it," she told him.

He went forward in a daze and scooped her close, bending over her with eyes that were suspiciously bright. "I knew it," he whispered huskily. "I knew!"

"I wish I had!" she exclaimed, hugging him hard. "All that wailing and gnashing of teeth, and for nothing!"

He chuckled. "What a nice surprise!"

"I thought so. Will you take me to lunch?" she added. "I want dill pickles and strawberry ice cream."

"Yuuuck!" Mrs. Mack said theatrically.

"Never you mind, Mrs. Mack, I'll take her home and feed her," Simon said placatingly. He glanced at his wife with a beaming smile. "We'll have Mrs. Lester fix us something. I want to enjoy looking at you in that outfit while we eat.''

She held his hand out the door and felt as if she had the world.

Later, after they arrived home, Mrs. Lester seated them at the dining-room table and brought in a nice lunch of cold cuts and omelets with decaffeinated coffee for Tira. She was smiling, too, because she was going with them to Austin.

''A baby and a husband who loves me, a terrific cook and housekeeper, and a mouseless house to leave behind,'' Tira said. ''What more could a woman ask?''

''Mouseless?'' Mrs. Lester asked.

''Yes, don't you remember?'' Tira asked gleefully. ''Cag got rid of the mouse while we were on our honeymoon and you were at your sister's.''

Mrs. Lester nodded. ''Got rid of the mouse. Mmmhmm.'' She went and opened the kitchen door and invited them to look at the cabinet. They peered in the door and there he was, the mouse, sitting on the counter with a cracker in his paws, blatantly nibbling away.

''I don't believe it!'' Tira burst out.

It got worse. Mrs. Lester went into the kitchen, held out her hand, and the mouse climbed into it.

''He's domesticated,'' she said proudly. ''I came in here the other morning and he was sitting on the cabinet. He didn't even try to run, so I held out my hand and he climbed into it. I had a suspicion, so I put him in a box and took him to the vet. The vet says that he isn't a wild mouse at all, he's somebody's pet mouse that got left behind and had to fend for himself. Obviously he belonged to the previous owners of this house. So I thought, if you don't mind, of course,'' she added kindly, "I'd keep him. He can come with us to Austin."

Tira looked at Simon and burst out laughing. The mouse, who had no interest whatsoever in human conversation, continued to nibble his cracker contentedly, safe in the hands of his new owner.

* * * * *

This March, those lovable
Long, Tall Texans return!
Celebrate the one year anniversary of
Silhouette Romance's Virgin Brides series with
Diana Palmer's delightful story

CALLAGHAN'S BRIDE

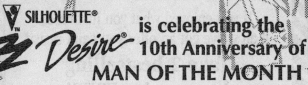

If you enjoyed what you just read,
then we've got an offer you can't resist!

Take 2 bestselling
love stories FREE!
Plus get a FREE surprise gift!

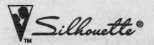

THE MacGREGORS ARE BACK!

#1 *New York Times* bestselling author

NORA ROBERTS

Presents...

THE MacGREGORS:
Alan—Grant

February 1999

Will Senator Alan MacGregor be able to help Shelby Campbell conquer her fear of his high-profile life-style? And will Grant Campbell and Gennie Grandeau find that their love is too strong to keep them apart? Find out by reading the exciting and touching *The MacGregors: Alan—Grant* by Nora Roberts.

Coming soon in
Silhouette Special Edition:

March 1999: THE PERFECT NEIGHBOR (SE#1232)

Also, watch for the MacGregor stories where it all began in the next exciting 2-in-1 volume!

April 1999: THE MacGREGORS: Daniel—Ian

Available at your favorite retail outlet, only from

Look us up on-line at: http://www.romance.net

PSNRAG

Based on the bestselling miniseries

FORTUNE'S Children™

A FORTUNE'S CHILDREN *Wedding:*
THE HOODWINKED BRIDE

by BARBARA BOSWELL

This March, the Fortune family discovers a twenty-six-year-old secret—beautiful Angelica Carroll *Fortune!* Kate Fortune hires Flynt Corrigan to protect the newest Fortune, and this jaded investigator soon finds this his most tantalizing—and tormenting—assignment to date....

Barbara Boswell's single title is just one of the captivating romances in Silhouette's exciting new miniseries, **Fortune's Children: The Brides,** featuring six special women who perpetuate a family legacy that is greater than mere riches!

Look for *The Honor Bound Groom,* by Jennifer Greene, when **Fortune's Children: The Brides** launches in Silhouette Desire in January 1999!

Available at your favorite retail outlet.

Silhouette®

COMING NEXT MONTH